★

Rhodes knocked.

There was no answer, but then he hadn't really been expecting one. He tried the doorknob, which turned easily in his hand. The door wasn't locked.

He opened it and went inside and called Faye's name. His voice echoed off the hardwood floors and bounced down the walls of the hallway.

There was no sign of the cats, but Rhodes knew they were there somewhere. He could feel his eyes beginning to itch already.

He walked down the short hall to the living room. Faye Knape was lying on the floor, her knees drawn up, her mouth open as if in a scream. Her forehead had been crushed. The cut-glass vase lay not far away, and the dried flowers were scattered on the floor.

★

"A solid addition to a long-running series."
—*Library Journal*

Previously published Worldwide Mystery titles by
BILL CRIDER

...A DANGEROUS THING
DEATH BY ACCIDENT
WINNING CAN BE MURDER

Forthcoming Worldwide Mystery title by
BILL CRIDER

THE EMPTY MANGER
(in MURDER, MAYHEM AND MISTLETOE)

A GHOST OF A CHANCE

BILL CRIDER

W🌐RLDWIDE.

TORONTO • NEW YORK • LONDON
AMSTERDAM • PARIS • SYDNEY • HAMBURG
STOCKHOLM • ATHENS • TOKYO • MILAN
MADRID • WARSAW • BUDAPEST • AUCKLAND

A GHOST OF A CHANCE

A Worldwide Mystery/September 2001

First published by St. Martin's Press, Incorporated.

ISBN 0-373-26396-1

Printed in U.S.A.

ONE

SHERIFF DAN RHODES didn't believe that the Blacklin County Jail was haunted. Neither did Lawton, the jailer.

But the dispatcher, Hack Jensen, said that it didn't make any difference what they believed.

"Those fellas back there in the cells believe it," he said. "And that's all that matters."

Lawton was leaning with one shoulder on the frame of the door that led to the lower cellblock. He had his hands clasped around the handle of the push broom that he held in front of him, right hand high, left hand low. He had a hard round stomach, and his olive-drab coveralls were a little strained across the middle.

It had been threatening rain all day. There was a flash of lightning outside, followed by a roll of thunder that rattled the windows.

"Good day for ghosts," Lawton said. "I remember that we had some dealin's with a haint not so long ago. In that college out there at Obert."

Rhodes wondered just what Lawton meant by *we*, since the way he remembered it, he was the only one who'd really been involved in that little incident. But Rhodes knew better than to say anything. If he did, he'd just hurt Lawton's feelings.

Hack, on the other hand, didn't seem to care whose feelings he hurt.

"Wasn't a ghost," he said. "Just a dead man."

Lawton shifted his weight on his short legs. "Dead

man's just about the next thing to a ghost, I guess. You could look it up on that computer of yours."

Hack was the dispatcher, and he had argued for years that the jail needed a computer. Now that he had one, he was inordinately proud of the things it could do. Lawton, who wasn't as enamored of technology as Hack was, liked to tease him about the new machine.

Hack grinned. "That's right. I could look it up, all right. If I wanted to."

"Right. It's all part of the information in that GCIC thing."

Hack stopped grinning. Rhodes knew why. Hack didn't like for anyone to make slighting remarks about the computer. At the beginning of the Obert college case, Hack had explained to Lawton about the computer's link to the National Crime Investigation Center, and Lawton had suggested that they tap into the Ghost Crime Investigation Center for some up-to-date information on what was going on in Obert. Hack hadn't thought it was funny.

"There's no such thing as the GCIC," Hack said now. "And you know it. But I can by God find out about jailhouse ghosts on the Internet."

The jail's Internet connection was new. Hack had suggested it to Rhodes, who had seen the value of it and had signed the jail up with a provider.

"All right, let's see what you can find," Lawton said, pushing his broom over to Hack's desk.

There was another rumble of thunder. The windows shook in their frames.

"Maybe I oughta unplug the computer," Hack said. "Wouldn't want to take a chance on it getting hit by lightning."

"You got one of those lightning spike protectors, don't you?" Lawton asked.

Hack nodded.

"Then what're you afraid of?"

"Nothing," Hack said. "Come on over here and have a look."

Lawton walked over to the dispatcher's desk. When the two of them were close together, they seemed to Rhodes to have a strong resemblance to the old comedy team of Abbott and Costello. Hack was tall, with slicked-back hair, a thin gray mustache, and a skeptical look, while Lawton had the smooth round face of an altar boy who was about to snatch the halo off a cherub.

"Just let me call up a search engine," Hack said.

"Is that like a car engine?" Lawton asked.

Hack didn't deign to answer. Rhodes got up from his desk and strolled over to the desk to watch Hack type "jail ghost" into the blank on the search engine's home page.

"Now watch this," Hack said, clicking on the go button.

He got only one response, a link to something called the Sydney Institute of Technology. Hack clicked on the link and a new screen appeared, revealing that the Sydney Institute was apparently holding classes in the old Darlinghurst Gaol, way Down Under.

"That supposed to be *goal?*" Lawton asked.

"It's the way they spell *jail* in Australia sometimes," Hack said. "See? It says it right there. J-a-i-l. They have to put that in for people who never took much English in school."

Lawton looked skeptical. "If they wanted to spell *jail,* why didn't they just do it in the first place? Doesn't make any sense to me."

"There's a lot of things don't make any sense to you," Hack said. "See what it says there? You can take a class

and find out about the convicts and gamblers." He gave
Lawton a significant look. "The gallows, too."

"Maybe so," Lawton said. "Don't see anything about
ghosts, though."

Rhodes figured it was time for him to step in. If he
didn't, the two old men would argue all day.

"It mentioned ghosts on the other page," he said.
"The first one we looked at."

Lawton shrugged. "Could be. Doesn't say anything
here, though, does it? Besides, who'd want to go to
classes in a jail if they didn't have to?"

"Maybe somebody that wanted to learn something,"
Hack said. "Somebody that didn't want to stay ignorant
all his life."

"Maybe we could offer some classes here," Lawton
said. "Tell 'em about that ghost we got."

"Good idea," Hack said. "We could build us a gallows and hang somebody as a demonstration."

It was pretty clear who he had in mind. So Rhodes
changed the subject.

"I haven't seen any ghost," he said.

"Me neither," Lawton said. "I don't believe in 'em,
myself. It's an ignorant superstition."

"Doesn't matter whether you believe in 'em or not,"
Hack said, and Rhodes had a strong feeling that this was
where he'd come in.

So before Hack could say anything about what "those
fellas back in the cells" believed, Rhodes said, "Has
anybody seen the ghost lately?"

Lawton straightened up. "Just Lank Rollins."

Rollins, whose habit of passing hot checks made him
a frequent resident of the jail cells, was the one who'd
started the whole thing. He claimed to have been sleeping
soundly in his bunk when he was awakened by a cold

breeze across his face. When he looked up, he saw a dark shadow moving across his cell. He tried to call out, but his throat "closed up like somebody stuck a rag down it." And when he tried to get out of the bunk, his blanket wrapped itself around him until he was "swaddled up like one of those Egyptian mummies."

That was the way Lawton had found him in the morning, lying rigidly in his wrappings, flat on his back on the bunk, unable to move.

Rhodes figured that Rollins had simply had a restless night and tangled himself in his blanket, not that it made any difference in the long run.

"Once one of them fellas gets an idea in his head," Hack said, "you can't get it out. And then ever'body else catches it."

Rhodes nodded. It was easy for rumors to get started in a jail, and the other five prisoners had picked up on the idea that a ghost was roaming around in their midst in about ten minutes after Rollins told Lawton the story. Before long, everyone was seeing or hearing the apparition.

One man swore he saw it in the showers. Another said that he heard it moaning in the corner of a vacant cell. And one said that it had walked right through the bars and stared at him.

Rhodes had asked what it looked like.

The man said, "A big black shadow," which was the way that everyone described it.

Rhodes thought they were seriously lacking in imagination.

"One thing I got to give that ghost credit for," Lawton said, leaning on the doorframe. "It's got all those fellas readin' their Bibles like crazy."

"Even Tobin," Hack said.

Andy Tobin, who had a drinking problem that landed him in jail fairly frequently, was the current jailhouse lawyer. Before the appearance of the ghost, he had been a consistent troublemaker, the kind of prisoner who spent most of his time filing grievances and going through lawbooks to prepare suits against the county, against the commissioners, against Rhodes, against Hack and Lawton, and, for all Rhodes knew, against the president and the Congress.

"Tobin's the worst one of all," Lawton said. "He hasn't had his nose out of that Bible for the past five days."

Rhodes went back to his desk. It was nice to know that the ghost was having a good effect on the prisoners' spiritual lives, which could probably use some improvement. But he was afraid any improvement that resulted would be only temporary. Before long, they'd find something else to distract them, and the ghost would be forgotten.

"The latest is, they're sayin' it's the ghost of old Ham Walker," Lawton said.

"Ham Walker," Hack said. "How in the world do they know about him?"

"Nearly everybody knows about him," Rhodes said. "I heard about him when I was just a kid."

It was a story that mothers in Blacklin County had for years told their children in an attempt to encourage better behavior. According to the most popular version of the tale, Walker had been found hanged in a cell only a few weeks after the jail opened more than seventy years before.

There was a persistent rumor that the hanging had not been a suicide. Walker supposedly had been assisted on his way to the afterlife by the sheriff and his deputies, all of whom had alibied each other. Rhodes didn't believe that part of the story in the least, though the part about Walker having hanged himself was true enough. It was in the jail records.

"Maybe that explains why the prisoners are bein' so well behaved," Hack said. "They're afraid you'll slip back there some night and hang ever' last one of 'em."

"Wouldn't be a bad idea," Lawton said. "I'm gettin' tired of seein' that Andy Tobin in here all the time."

He was about to expand on that idea when the telephone rang.

Hack answered and then listened for a while to someone with an excited voice that Rhodes could hear all the way across the room, though he couldn't make out the words. Hack wrote down all the information he was given and assured the caller that the sheriff was on the way.

"On the way to where?" Rhodes asked when Hack hung up.

"To the cemetery. That was Clyde Ballinger on the line. He says there's a dead man in one of the graves out there."

"Now, there's a surprise," Lawton said.

TWO

THE RAIN STARTED coming down hard just as Rhodes left the jail, and he ran to the county car with his raincoat flapping around his legs.

The sky was black as night until another bolt of lightning flashed, backlighting the jail and making it look to Rhodes a little like the Castle of Frankenstein. The slam of the car door was drowned out by a whip-crack of thunder.

Rhodes started the car, then turned on the wipers and the headlights. The wipers sluiced water off the windshield, and Rhodes wheeled off toward the cemetery with his headlights reflecting off the slick and shiny street.

To get there he had to drive through downtown Clearview. As depressing as the day was already, a drive through downtown wasn't going to improve things.

For one thing, there wasn't much of a downtown left. Rhodes looked out at the buildings from the car. Most of them were deserted, and a couple had recently collapsed as a result of age and neglect. The noise, according to those who'd heard it, had been louder than the thunder that was presently booming overhead. One of the walls had fallen across the sidewalk and into the street, blocking passage for two days until the rubble could be cleared away. Rhodes suspected that the buildings would never even be repaired, much less restored.

Clearview had been a thriving place when Rhodes was a boy, or so it had seemed to him. He could remember Saturday afternoons when the sidewalks of the main street were so crowded that you could hardly walk. Everybody was in town, including all the farmers who had then lived in the surrounding countryside.

On the street corner near one of the drugstores there was always a skinny Pentecostal evangelist who wore a suit and tie even in the middle of the summer and preached to the passersby through a cheap amplifier that sat on the hood of his car. Hardly anyone ever stopped to listen to him, but he stayed there all day, preaching until well after dark, since the crowd didn't begin to thin out until the stores closed around eight o'clock.

There had been three movie theaters in Clearview then, three five-and-dime stores, five or six department stores, four drugstores, a shoe store, four grocery stores, a furniture store, two jewelry stores, a bookstore, and a couple of cafés, one of which served the best hot roast beef sandwiches Rhodes had ever eaten. He remembered the brown gravy that covered the open-face sandwich, and the mashed potatoes with more brown gravy that were served on the side.

Now there were no cafés downtown, and no theaters at all. The skinny evangelist was long gone. If you wanted to see a movie, you rented a video or drove to a city; if you wanted to see an evangelist, you just turned on your TV set. And if you wanted a hot roast beef sandwich, well, in that case you were completely out of luck. As far as Rhodes knew, there was no place left in Texas that served them.

There were a couple of drugstores in town now, but they were nothing like the ones Rhodes remembered, places where he had bought hand-packed ice-cream cones, comic books, cherry phosphates, and chocolate malts that you could turn upside down without spilling a drop.

There was still one grocery store near downtown, but no jewelry stores, furniture stores, or shoe stores. There was no bookstore. There were two department stores, but they were barely hanging on. The place had almost become a ghost town, which Rhodes supposed was appropriate, considering that the jail was now being haunted.

That didn't mean there was no life or commercial activity in Clearview. There was plenty, and most of it was at the Wal-Mart, located out on the highway, where its parking lot was full at all hours. It seemed to draw people like flypaper drew flies. Not that anyone would remember what flypaper was.

Rhodes drove past the collapsed buildings. One of them was mostly just a pile of rubble. The streetlights were on, and in the ghostly blue glow the building looked as if it had been hit by a bomb. Bricks were still lying all over the sidewalk, which was blocked off by a single strand of yellow plastic with the word caution printed on it in black every few inches.

When Rhodes had been much younger, the building had housed a tire and appliance store. He could remember the strong smell of the rubber when he stood in the back of the store to watch Noah Elarton balance tires, mark them with chalk, and hammer the lead weights onto the rims.

There was no one standing anywhere around now, and Rhodes didn't even see any other cars on the street.

He drove on to the cemetery and went straight in through the wide-open gates. The road was lined with crepe myrtle trees that had been severely trimmed. They'd be blooming in another few months, but now they were stark and bare. The cedars farther from the road were green, and so were the oaks, but they looked black in the gloom of the day. A lightning flash threw shadows on the road, and thunder shook the car.

Rhodes didn't know exactly where the grave he was looking for was located, but he thought it would be easy to find. And it was. There was a canopy set up off to the right, and Rhodes turned in that direction.

He stopped the car behind a black Cadillac from which Clyde Ballinger emerged, raising a huge black umbrella over his head. Rhodes got out and joined him.

"Nice day," Ballinger said.

Ballinger wore a black suit, a white shirt, a black tie, and shiny black shoes that had just a little bit of mud on them. He was smiling and cheerful, as he usually was, and he didn't look like an undertaker, or a funeral director, as they were called these days. Or maybe that was out of fashion, too. For all Rhodes knew they were called "grief managers."

"Perfect," Rhodes said. "It just doesn't get any better than this."

A drop of cold rain got under his raincoat collar and rolled down his neck. Rhodes hated umbrellas, and he hated hats. He thought he was probably the only sheriff in all of Texas' two hundred and fifty-four counties who didn't own a Stetson. Usually he didn't regret that fact. Today, he did.

"Let's go see what the trouble is," he said.

They walked across the wet grass to the dark green canopy. The bottoms of Rhodes's pants legs got heavier with every step.

The ground under the canopy had been spread with fake grass of an odd light green color more likely to be found on the floor of a domed stadium than anywhere outside. It was just as wet as the real thing, however.

A nearby mound of dirt was also discreetly covered

with the fake grass, but Rhodes could smell the rooty
odor of newly dug earth. Folding chairs were lined up
for the mourners to sit in. The wind flapped the edges of
the canopy, but at least it was a little drier under there.
The rain pounded on the canvas over their heads.

"I came out here to check on things," Ballinger said.
He folded the umbrella and shook off some of the rain-
drops. "The way I always do. That's when I found him."

"Who?" Rhodes asked.

"Whoever's in that grave. I couldn't tell who it was,
and I didn't want to find out. I figure that's what the
county pays you the big bucks to do."

Rhodes stepped over to the grave and looked. There
was a man lying face down at the bottom.

Lightning ripped across the sky and thunder rolled.
Rhodes felt for just a second as if he'd stumbled onto the
set of an old Universal horror movie from the 1940s. He
looked out through the rain, half expecting to see Lon
Chaney, Jr., slink across the graveyard and skulk behind
an obelisk to wait for the rising of the full moon.

He didn't see Chaney, but he did see someone.

The cemetery was on a hill, and as Rhodes looked
down toward the bottom, past all the tombstones, he saw
someone, or some*thing,* run out of the trees. Because of
the rain and the sooty darkness of the sky, he couldn't
be sure who or what it was. It flickered out of the trees
and into a clearing, followed closely by another shadowy
figure, and then the two of them disappeared into the
trees again.

"This is supposed to be Travis McCoy's grave," Ballinger said. "His wife requested a hand-dug grave, and
that's what she got. We did the job and got everything
set up late yesterday because of the weather forecast."

"Do you see anything down there?" Rhodes asked, pointing toward the clearing.

"Just the railroad tracks, and they've been there since long before I was born. Why?"

"I thought I saw somebody run out of the trees on this side of the tracks."

"Not in this weather. Who'd be out on a day like this? Except us, and we have to be here, or at least you do. Anyway, I was telling you about this grave. It's for Travis McCoy."

McCoy had been a retired schoolteacher. Rhodes hadn't known him very well, though the newspaper had said he was very popular with his students. Rhodes looked at the stone at the head of the grave. The inscription on one side of it said:

TRAVIS MCCOY
June 23, 1919
March 1, 1999

The other side of the stone read:

ELIZABETH GATLIN MCCOY
January 5, 1920

Second date pending, Rhodes thought, not certain what was making him so morbid. Maybe it was the ghost in the jail.

Or maybe it was the dead man who was lying there in the wrong grave.

Rhodes wondered how he was going to get down in the grave and have a look at the body. The weather had already played havoc with the crime scene, but he didn't want to do anymore damage than necessary.

"The McCoy funeral's at two," Ballinger said. "Not that I'm rushing you, but it's already past eleven o'clock."

"Don't worry," Rhodes said. "I'm not rushing."

He sat on the edge of the grave, wondering how he'd ever get the mud out of his pants and raincoat, and slid down. He managed to land on his feet at the bottom. His shoes slipped on the slick earth, but he was able to avoid stepping on the body, which was that of a short, thin man wearing jeans, leather hiking shoes, and a camo windbreaker.

As far as Rhodes could see there were no clues lying there, so he turned the body over and looked at its face.

"It's Ty Berry," he said, without surprise.

"Oh, Lord," Ballinger said. "Tell me he died of a heart attack."

"I could tell you that, but it wouldn't be the truth."

"Why not?"

"Because somebody shot him," Rhodes said.

THREE

TY BERRY WAS, or had been, the president of the Clearview Sons and Daughters of Texas, a group devoted to the preservation of landmarks and the history of Clearview and Blacklin County. Berry himself had been interested in every aspect of the county's past. No detail had been too trivial or obscure for his attention.

Rhodes had attended a recent meeting of the county commissioners at which Berry had been accused by one of them of having far too much love for anything in the county that was old and useless.

Berry had given him a cold look and said, "There are some old, useless men I don't love. Some of them I don't even like very much."

The commissioner hadn't been amused, and he hadn't done much in the way of supporting Berry's latest project, which had been increasing the protection of all the cemeteries in Blacklin county, including the one located within the Clearview city limits.

Berry had brought the presidents of twelve different cemetery associations with him to the meeting. Each of them represented one of the small private cemeteries that were scattered over the county, and all had the same complaint: someone had been looting their cemeteries, stealing statues, urns, and even obelisks, stelae, and tombstones.

The commissioners were skeptical. Some of them appeared to think that the losses were due to something like the natural deterioration of materials.

"If people stole that kind of stuff, what would they do with it?" Jay Bowman had asked.

Bowman was a big, red-faced man who represented Precinct Four, which contained three of the cemeteries represented by the association presidents who were there.

"Sell it," Berry said.

"Those markers all have names on them," Bowman said. "Who'd buy them?"

"They sand off the names and dates," Berry said. "Then they sell them at flea markets."

Bowman shook his head as if he were having a hard time believing what he was hearing.

"I don't get it. Who'd want anything like that?"

"You'd be surprised," Berry said.

"Probably. But what about that other stuff you were telling us about? Urns, statues, things like that. People really buy that?"

"Yes," Berry said. "But not always at flea markets. Some of those items are valuable as antiques. People even use them to decorate their homes."

"Cemetery chic," said Jerry Purcell from Precinct Three.

Purcell was tall and skinny and had a face webbed by a thousand wrinkles, give or take ten or twelve. His fingers worked constantly as he sat at the table because when he wasn't smoking a cigarette, he couldn't figure out what to do with his hands. And there was no smoking allowed in the meeting room, or any of the rooms in county buildings.

"You could call it that," Berry said.

"I can see how people could take things from the county cemeteries," Bowman said. "But the one in Clearview's right in town. It has gates on it. And a caretaker."

"Makes no difference," Berry said. "The gates are never locked, day or night. I've never even seen them closed. And the caretaker doesn't live there anymore. There hasn't been anyone living on the grounds there in years. People go in and out at all hours."

Rhodes knew that was true. The deputies tried to patrol the place, especially on weekends, to keep out the local teenagers who found it a nice, quiet place to park. That was one thing that hadn't changed in Clearview. Rhodes could remember having parked there a time or two himself, a long time ago.

"So what do you want us to do about all this?" Purcell asked.

"I want you to have the sheriff put a stop to it," Berry said, which was exactly what Rhodes had been expecting.

The trouble was, it wouldn't be possible, not unless he got very lucky or unless the commissioners hired ten or eleven more deputies, neither of which was the least bit likely. There were so many little cemeteries sprinkled around the county that it would be impossible even to visit all of them on any particular night, and leaving a deputy on watch at one of them for any extended period of time would deprive some other part of the county of an expected patrol.

That was the way the commissioners saw it, too, and Berry had been quite upset. But he'd behaved himself well. He hadn't shouted or made any other demands. Instead he'd simply said that he'd patrol the cemeteries himself. Six of the cemetery association presidents had said they'd do the same, and the other six had promised that, while they wouldn't be going out on patrol themselves, they had people in the association who'd be more than glad to do so.

Rhodes knew that at least some of those who set themselves up as cemetery guardians would be armed, most of them legally so, thanks to the fact that it was now legal to carry concealed firearms in Texas, just as long as the carrier had been through the proper course of education. Rhodes figured that was just what the county needed: cemetery vigilantes.

He'd recommended that the sheriff's office be given a little time to try to put a stop to things, but that hadn't satisfied Berry.

"You haven't done anything in the last six months," he said. "In six more, there won't be a statue or an urn left in the county. In a year, there might not be any gravestones."

Rhodes thought that was a pretty big exaggeration, and he was sure Berry knew it was, too. Not that it made any difference.

"It's a free country," Berry said. "At least it used to be. If we want to drive past the cemeteries at night, we have a right to do it."

Rhodes couldn't argue with that, or he hadn't thought he could at the time.

Now that it was too late, he wished he had. Maybe if he'd argued, Berry wouldn't be lying there at his feet in an open grave that was meant for someone else.

Rhodes looked at Berry's face. The worry line that Rhodes remembered being between his eyebrows was still there, but right at the top of it was a small hole, probably made by a .22-caliber bullet. There was no exit wound. A .22 was likely just to rattle around inside the skull, scrambling the brain like a skillet full of eggs until it slowed to a stop.

Rhodes scanned the ground around the body, but he didn't see anything that looked like a clue to who had killed Berry, or why. He bent down and lifted the body to look beneath it. Berry's body was light as a child's.

There was nothing on the ground, so Rhodes lowered the body and looked up at Ballinger.

"Help me out of here," he said, putting up a dirty hand.

Ballinger backed away a step. "You might pull me down in there with you. I have some men on the way. They'll help you out."

Rhodes didn't mind the wait. He used the time to examine Berry's clothing and the slick walls of the grave. He didn't find anything resembling a clue, though he did locate Berry's wallet and pickup keys, both of which seemed to rule out robbery as a motive. Rhodes could see at the top edge of the grave a place where the dirt was disturbed. Berry had probably been standing there when he'd been shot.

After about five minutes Rhodes heard a vehicle pull to a stop nearby. Two doors slammed, and two men came over to the grave.

"The sheriff's down there," Ballinger told them. "Along with that body I told you about. He needs a little help to get out. The sheriff, not the body."

One of the men stepped over and looked down at Rhodes.

"Hey, Sheriff," he said. "Who else is that down there with you?"

Rhodes didn't recognize the man. He said, "It's Ty Berry. How about getting us out of here?"

"Him first," the man said.

Rhodes lifted Berry up easily enough, and Ballinger's two helpers pulled him up to ground level, where they laid him on a gurney they'd brought with them. They'd worked for Ballinger long enough to be almost casual about it.

When they had things arranged to their satisfaction, they returned to the grave and helped Rhodes climb out. By the time he reached the top, his shoes were covered with mud, which he tracked on the fake grass.

"Don't worry about it," Ballinger said. "I'll get it cleaned off before the funeral."

His helpers pushed the gurney over to the hearse. They'd put the body in a plastic bag, so it wasn't getting rained on. Rhodes could hear the rain popping against the plastic.

"You want me to call Dr. White?" Ballinger asked.

White did autopsies for the county. Rhodes told Ballinger to make the call.

"What about Berry's family?"

Berry had been a lifelong bachelor, but he probably had relatives who would have to be notified. Rhodes dreaded making the call, but since he was the one who'd have to find out who the relatives were, he was the logical one to do the calling.

"I'll take care of that part," Rhodes said.

"What about the McCoy funeral?" Ballinger wanted to know. "Can we go ahead with it?"

Rhodes didn't think there was anything in the grave that would help him, and there was no trace of any other evidence that he could see. There was no .22 casing lying on the fake grass, no footprints except for those left by Berry as he fell, no sign that anyone had been there at all.

"Sure," Rhodes said. "Go ahead."

"All right. If you say so. I hope Miz McCoy isn't too upset by all this."

That wasn't Rhodes's problem, and he was sure Ballinger was capable of dealing with it. Then something else occurred to him, something he should have thought of earlier.

"I wonder where Berry's truck is," he said.

"I didn't think about that," Ballinger said. "He had to get here somehow, though. Maybe he rode with somebody. Or maybe he walked."

"I'll have a look around," Rhodes said. "You can go on and take care of Mrs. McCoy. And thanks for giving me a call about this."

"Just doing my duty as a citizen."

Ballinger raised his umbrella and stepped out from under the tent. He got into his Cadillac and followed the black hearse as it drove away through the rain.

FOUR

RHODES DIDN'T OWN a Stetson, but he did have an old fishing hat that he kept in the trunk of the county car in case of emergency. The rain hadn't slacked off at all, and that was enough of an emergency for Rhodes. He opened the trunk and rummaged under a set of jumper cables. After a second, he dragged out the crumpled hat and jammed it firmly down on his head.

He looked back down the hill, but no mysterious figures slunk out of the trees.

Maybe I was just imagining things, he thought, though it had certainly seemed he'd seen something down there.

Whatever it had been, he didn't have time to wonder about it now. He sloshed off through the rain to have a look around the cemetery, which he'd always found an interesting place. He could see why Ty Berry didn't want anything to happen to it.

Or anything more. Off to Rhodes's right there was a mildew-streaked pedestal on which a marble angel had once stood. The angel was no longer there, and it hadn't flown away by itself. It had received a little help from whoever was looting the county's graveyards.

Rhodes brushed rain off his forehead. Farther up the road there was a semicircle of Greek columns that indicated the area where the members of the Pooley family were buried. The family had made its money during the oil years, but there were no Pooleys left in Clearview now, not counting those who were under the ground. The ones who were still alive had all moved to Dallas and

Houston, where they lived in big houses, drove big cars, and hardly ever returned to the place where the family fortune had been made.

Rhodes figured he'd be hearing from some of them the next time they were in town, however, since within the last few months someone had stolen a couple of urns and a concrete bench from the Pooley tract.

Rhodes turned right and walked toward the place where the caretaker's house had once stood. It had been replaced years ago by a concrete-block storage building that held groundskeeping equipment and supplies: mowers, weed whackers, tree trimmers, fertilizer, weed killer, hoses.

Rhodes looked around as he passed the tombstones. Some of them were mottled and worn, with dates from the previous century, and there was quite a group from 1918-1919; the flu epidemic hadn't spared even small towns in Texas.

Some of the newer stones had artistic touches that hadn't been thought of in those days. On one of them was a picture of bluebonnets. On another was a picture of a man fishing from a bass boat.

Rhodes wouldn't mind having one like that for himself, except that it wouldn't represent him very accurately these days. As much as he liked fishing, he hardly ever got to go.

When he reached the storage building, he walked around behind it where a blue Ford pickup was parked. Rhodes had thought it might be there. There was nowhere else in the cemetery to conceal a vehicle.

There was nothing out of the ordinary about the truck, but Rhodes was sure it belonged to Ty Berry. He'd seen Berry driving it often enough.

Rhodes looked carefully at the ground all around the

truck. He found an old rusty bottle cap, a bent nail that was even rustier, and nothing else.

There was nothing in the rear of the truck, either, except a thick rubber mat to keep the paint from getting scratched when something was being hauled back there. Rhodes lifted the mat. There was no killer lurking under it, so he dropped it back down.

Rhodes looked through the window into the cab of the pickup. Berry had been a neat man, and the interior of the pickup was very clean. There was a litter bag hanging from a knob on the dash, and there were a couple pieces of paper in it. Rhodes couldn't see what they were.

He tried the door. It was unlocked, and Rhodes let himself in, though he almost hated to open the door and get water all over the interior, possibly messing up the crime scene. He felt even worse about getting inside with his muddy shoes, but he was tired of being in the rain. His hat was already soaked, and his socks were squishing when he walked.

So he got in the truck. The rain popped against the roof like number two buckshot, and Rhodes took the papers out of the litter bag, holding them carefully by the edges. He'd never solved a case with the help of fingerprints, but there was always a first time.

One of the pieces of paper was a grocery list. The words were written in small, neat, precise cursive script, the kind of handwriting that Rhodes had always admired but had never been able to master. The list included black pepper, ground beef, onions, potatoes, hamburger buns.

Rhodes almost smiled. Berry was a man after his own heart, or at least after his own appetite. Appetite was one thing Berry wouldn't have to be worrying about anymore.

Rhodes dropped the list back in the litter bag and removed the other paper. It was written in the same neat hand and said, "A.D. 11."

Rhodes didn't know what that meant. Maybe it referred to some important historical event in the year A.D. 11. Rhodes tried to think of what the event could have been. Had the Romans taken over in Egypt about that time? He wasn't sure. He could recognize Greek columns easily enough, but when he'd been in school, he'd always done better in American history than in the history of the world.

He dropped the paper back in the litter bag and looked around the rest of the pickup's interior. There was nothing of interest in sight, so Rhodes opened the glove compartment.

There were no gloves inside it. The compartment held a road map of the United States, a map of Texas, and a map of Blacklin County with all the private cemeteries marked in red ink. Berry, or someone, had inked in the names.

There was also another list. It had most likely been printed out on a computer. It was dated the previous day, and it had on it all the items that had been stolen from the various cemeteries around the county. Rhodes would have one of his deputies check to see if there was anything new missing from the Clearview cemetery. If there was, that might mean that whoever had been doing the looting might be responsible for Berry's death.

Rhodes put the maps and the list back where he'd found them and got out of the pickup, leaving the litter bag inside. He didn't have much to show for his search. He could have one of the deputies do a more thorough job after the rain stopped, if it ever did, but he didn't have much hope that she'd turn up anything more.

He left the keys under the floor mat, got out of the

pickup, and squished back to the county car. When he was inside, he radioed Hack and said, "I'm going to look around here a little more, and then I'm going home to put on some dry clothes."

"What about Ty Berry?" Hack asked. "You gonna call his cousin in Austin?"

Rhodes should have realized that Hack would already know about Berry. It was impossible to keep anything a secret in a small town. And he should also have known that Hack would know who Berry's relatives were. Hack knew more about most people in Blacklin County than they knew themselves.

"I'll call," Rhodes said. "Get his number, and I'll come by after I've changed."

"It's a her," Hack said. "He's got an uncle somewhere, too."

"The cousin can make that call," Rhodes said.

"You gonna tell me what happened?"

Rhodes knew that Hack wanted the whole story in order to keep ahead of Lawton. Both men liked to be the first with details. But the sheriff wasn't going to broadcast anything on the radio. There were too many people who had nothing better to do than listen in on their scanners.

"I'll tell you when I get there," Rhodes said. "Have there been any other calls?"

"Nothin' important. Some goats got out on the road down close to Thurston, and somebody hit one of 'em. Nobody's hurt, though. Except the goat. Ruth Grady's down there."

Ruth was one of the deputies. She could handle just about any situation that came up. A dead goat and a dented car wouldn't be a problem.

"What about the ghost?" he asked.

"Nobody's seen him lately," Hack said. "Looks like he'd turn up today if he ever did, the weather we're havin'. It's not good for much of anything 'cept maybe ghosts."

"Maybe he's gone for good."

"Maybe." Hack didn't sound convinced. "You gonna get back here pretty soon?"

"Give me an hour," Rhodes said.

FIVE

RHODES DROVE OUT OF the cemetery and down the street to the highway. He turned right and headed for the railroad overpass, but just before he got there, he turned off on a one-lane gravel road that ran down beside the overpass and then turned to parallel the railroad tracks. There were soft spots in the road where the gravel had been washed away, and Rhodes had to be careful not to let the car slide off into the ditch.

When he came to a spot near where he'd seen the figures running out of the trees, he stopped the car. There was no place to pull off the road, but he didn't think he had to worry about traffic. Hardly anyone ever used the road, and it wasn't likely that anyone was going to try driving on it in the rain.

Rhodes put on his soggy hat and got out of the car. He'd have to cross the ditch to get to the trees, and the ditch was half full of water. As wet as he was already, he might as well just walk through it, but he didn't want to do that. So he decided to jump it.

Once, a long time ago, jumping across a couple feet of running water wouldn't have been worth a second thought. These days, however, it was a different story. One of the things Rhodes didn't like about getting older was the discovery that doing things he'd once taken for granted had become a good bit more difficult. And it wasn't his fault; it wasn't as if he'd asked for his body to deteriorate.

Thinking about it didn't help anything, so he took a

couple of halfhearted running steps and jumped the ditch. The good news was that he made it. The bad news was that the landing jarred his knees so hard that he stumbled forward for several feet and nearly fell flat on his face. His pulse raced, and he had to wave his arms to maintain his balance. When he got his momentum under control, he stood still for a minute to let his heartbeat get back to normal. He hoped no one had been watching.

After a while, he walked up to the trees. The ground was muddier than it had been up on the hill in the cemetery, and now and then his shoes made little sucking noises as he picked up his feet.

When he got into the trees, Rhodes listened to the sound of the rain crackling on the dead leaves. He didn't hear anything else for a few seconds, and then he heard a faraway train whistle as an engine came to a crossing. The whistle grew louder with each crossing the train passed, and before long the cars began passing by. Rhodes watched them go, listening to the familiar clickety-clack of the wheels on the tracks.

There had once been a depot in Clearview, and trains had made regular stops there, though that had been before Rhodes's time. There were no stops now, of course, and the depot had been razed when Rhodes was just a boy.

The train passed by, and soon the only sound Rhodes could hear was that made by the rain. He wondered if he'd imagined the two figures darting across the clearing.

He walked out of the trees and into the clearing. The rain was still falling, though it was slackening up some. Rhodes looked for tracks in the grass, but he couldn't find any. Grass didn't take tracks well, and the rain didn't help. The only thing he found was an old cellophane-wrapped package that had held Camel cigarettes. It was empty and the colors were faded. It didn't look as if it had been dropped there at anytime in the recent past.

He stuck the pack in the pocket of his raincoat and looked at the trees on the other side of the clearing. They went on for about a quarter of a mile. It would take a long time to search through them, more time than he had, but he could at least take a look.

He didn't find a thing, just dead leaves underfoot and rain dripping down from above. There were no houses within half a mile of the trees, and from what Rhodes could see, there was no activity at any of them.

He squished and squashed his way back to the county car, jumping the ditch again, and then drove along the road until he came to a place where he could turn around. There was nothing in the fields along the road, and not a single car had passed since Rhodes had been in the vicinity.

His raincoat was drenched, and his clothes were sticking to him. He had made a cold, damp spot where he sat in the front seat of the county car.

He decided it was time to go home.

THE RAIN HAD finally stopped by the time Rhodes got home, but it was still dark and overcast. There was no more thunder and lightning, however, and Rhodes figured that the weather front had moved on to the south.

He parked the county car in the driveway and checked in the back yard to make sure that his main dog, Speedo, whose real name was Mr. Earl, was doing all right. Speedo poked his nose out of the Styrofoam igloo that served as his doghouse and barked once in greeting, but elected to stay inside. Rhodes didn't blame him.

As he reached his back door, Rhodes heard a frenzied barking from inside the house.

"All right, Yancey," Rhodes said. "Hold it down. It's only me."

The barking continued. Yancey, a Pomeranian that Rhodes had acquired in the course of an investigation, was fiercely protective of his territory. Or else he just liked to bark. Rhodes wasn't sure which.

Rhodes had been afraid that Speedo might consider Yancey an intruder, which would have been unfair to Yancey, considering that Rhodes had also acquired Speedo in the course of an investigation. Somehow, he seemed to accumulate dogs; it wasn't a deliberate strategy.

At any rate, Speedo and Yancey had gotten along just fine, maybe because Yancey was a house dog and Speedo was a yard dog. But even when they were together, they seemed to have a high old time. Yancey didn't appear to notice that he was about a tenth of Speedo's size. For that matter, Speedo didn't seem to notice, either.

Rhodes opened the door and stepped inside. Yancey swarmed around his ankles, nipping at them and barking.

"Knock it off," Rhodes said. "I'm the master here. You're the dog."

Yancey ignored him, as always, but soon got tired of barking. He walked away a short distance and sat down by the washing machine, staring at Rhodes suspiciously.

Rhodes took off his raincoat and draped it over a chair back. Then he undressed and dropped his clothes in a sodden heap on the floor by the washing machine. Yancey barked at the heap.

"Hush," Rhodes said, heading for the bathroom.

Yancey stopped barking, which was a relief. He turned from the pile of clothes and followed Rhodes.

Rhodes toweled off and went into the bedroom to get

dry clothes. He had just finished dressing when the phone rang. Rhodes picked it up.

"Hello," he said.

"Sheriff? This is James Allen."

Allen was one of the county commissioners, probably Rhodes's best friend among the group. He'd had almost nothing to say at the meeting where Ty Berry had appeared, but Rhodes knew exactly what the subject of this call would be.

"I hear that Ty Berry got himself killed in the Clearview Cemetery," Allen said.

"You heard right," Rhodes told him, no more surprised that Allen knew than that Hack had known. By now, probably half the county knew.

"You know what people are going to say about us," James said.

Rhodes knew that the *us* referred to both the commissioners and to Rhodes himself, and he knew pretty much what people would be saying: that the commissioners should have hired some deputies to patrol the cemeteries; that because they hadn't, Rhodes or one of the deputies should have been there anyway; and that because of what hadn't been done, Ty Berry's death was all the fault of the commissioners and the sheriff's department.

None of that was necessarily true, but that was what people would say. And after they'd said it enough, they'd believe it.

"I know," Rhodes said.

"Well, what are you going to do about it?"

"I'm going to find out who killed Ty Berry."

"And how soon are you going to do that?"

"As soon as I can."

"I hope that won't be too long," Allen said.

"So do I," Rhodes told him.

SIX

AFTER ALLEN HUNG UP, Rhodes went into the kitchen. Yancey was sitting expectantly by the table.

"You'll just have to eat out of your bowl," Rhodes said. "Besides, you wouldn't like what I'm going to eat."

Rhodes didn't much like it himself, as far as that went. His wife, Ivy, had recently discovered a form of fake baloney made of some kind of vegetable mixture. Rhodes suspected there was tofu in there somewhere. However, there was no fat, and Ivy had insisted that a sandwich made from it tasted just as good as the real thing. It didn't to Rhodes, and the low-fat Miracle Whip didn't, either. Put a slice of fake cheese, also made with tofu, on the sandwich, and Rhodes supposed you had a really healthy lunch, but one that he found about as tasty as the afternoon newspaper.

For just a second or two, he thought longingly about a hot roast beef sandwich and how good it would taste. But since he couldn't have one, he made the healthy sandwich of vegetable products, ate it, and washed it down with tap water. As far as he knew, there was nothing fattening at all in tap water. He'd tried diet Dr Pepper, but he couldn't get used to it. For his money, Dr Pepper without the sugar just wasn't Dr Pepper.

When he was done with the sandwich, he went out on the porch and dropped the wet clothes in the washer. Yancey was over on the other side of the porch eating, which he enjoyed even more than he did barking. He paid no attention at all to Rhodes, who turned on the washer, put in the soap, and told Yancey it was time to go outside for a while.

Yancey wasn't enthusiastic. While Rhodes held the door open, he looked out at the puddles of water with what appeared to be vast suspicion.

"Fine," Rhodes said. "If you don't want to go, you don't have to."

Yancey immediately bounded outside, yipping and running over to Speedo's igloo. Speedo came out, and they both charged around the yard chasing one another and splashing through every puddle they could find. Some of them they splashed through twice.

When Yancey was finished with his business, Rhodes let him back in the house. Speedo hung around expectantly, as if hoping that Rhodes would stick around for a romp. Rhodes apologized for not having the time, and left.

BACK AT THE JAIL, Rhodes had to tell Hack and Lawton all about Ty Berry, though they already knew most of the story.

"I'll bet it was that Faye Knape who killed him," Hack said when Rhodes was finished.

Faye Knape was the immediate past president of the Clearview Historical Society, a group that was often in conflict with Ty Berry's Sons and Daughters of Texas. Both groups wanted the same things, but they couldn't always agree on how to get them. In fact, they could hardly ever agree on anything at all other than their basic goals. Rhodes sometimes thought that the disagreements were a result of each group's desire to get the credit for whatever gains in historical preservation were made in the county.

Recently the two groups had at last found something to bring them together: the cemetery issue. Though none of the Historical Society members had been at the commissions' meeting, they had written a letter to the Clearview *Herald* expressing their support for the Sons and Daughters' campaign to save the cemeteries.

There was only one problem: Faye Knape didn't agree with the rest of her organization's members. She thought that Ty Berry was, as she put it, "grandstanding to get attention." She didn't believe that the looting was as serious as he said it was, she didn't think that the county should be wasting its time and money on extra patrols, and she even hinted that Ty Berry might be ransacking the graveyards himself, just to draw attention to the Sons and Daughters.

"I'll bet what happened is this," Hack continued. "Old Faye went out there to the cemetery to confront Ty, and he stood right up to her. She wouldn't like that. So she shot him."

"Don't sound likely to me," Lawton said. "She's a good-sized woman. She wouldn't have to shoot him. She could've just squashed him like a fly."

"It's *flea*," Hack said. "Squashed him like a *flea*. Ever'body knows you can't squash a fly."

"Can't squash a flea, either," Lawton said. "You ever try it? Those boogers are unsquashable, unless you get 'em between two hard places. Sometimes they can get away even then. I remember an old dog I had—"

"We ain't talkin' about your old dog, and we ain't talkin' about fleas," Hack said. "We're talkin' about a man that's been shot. And from what I hear, he was shot with a .22. Is that right, Sheriff?"

Rhodes admitted that the .22 was a possibility but not a certainty.

"And by the way," he said, "where do you get all your information, anyhow?"

"I got my sources," Hack said. "We ain't talkin' about that, though. We're talking about a .22. Woman's gun. Ever'body knows that."

"Not all the time," Lawton said. "Those big-time hit men for the Mafia, they like that .22 Colt's Woodsman."

"Mafia?" Hack was incredulous. "Big-time hit men? You been rentin' *The Godfather* again, am I right? That part three really bites the moose if you ask me."

"Nobody asked you, though," Lawton said. "And anyway, that part three's not as bad as—"

"That's enough," Rhodes said, knowing that if he didn't stop them they could go on all day like that. He was pretty sure they did it just to drive him crazy. "You can forget about the Mafia. I don't think they're involved in this. Blacklin County's a little too far out of the way of things to get them interested. And you'd better forget about Miss Knape, too, at least until I've done some investigating. We don't go accusing people of murder on the basis of suspicion."

Lawton leaned on his broom, grinning widely, and didn't say a word.

"Humpf," Hack said. "Well, if you don't think it was Miz Knape who shot Berry, who do you think it was?"

"I don't know," Rhodes said. "Maybe it was whoever's been taking things from the cemeteries. Maybe not. That's what I'm going to find out."

"I bet the commissioners want you to find out this afternoon," Hack said. "If not sooner."

For a second Rhodes wondered if Hack had tapped his home phone, but he knew that wasn't the case. Hack just knew what the representatives of county government were like.

"You're right," he said. "Did you get me the number of Berry's cousin?"

Hack handed him a piece of paper. "Here it is."

"Thanks," Rhodes said. "Now, if you two will hold it down, I have a phone call to make."

SEVEN

THE CALL WAS JUST as bad as Rhodes had thought it would be. He wasn't good at dealing with the grief of others, and though Ty Berry and his cousin obviously hadn't been close, there were still some difficult moments. Rhodes was glad to hang up the telephone. After trying to clear his mind for a couple of minutes, he put on his reading glasses and started working on the report of Berry's death.

Almost as soon as he did, another call came in. Hack took it and began smirking at Rhodes before he'd exchanged ten words with the caller. Rhodes had an uncomfortable feeling he knew what that meant.

Sure enough, Hack put his hand over the mouthpiece and said, "It's Miz Wilkie. She wants to talk to you."

Mrs. Wilkie had once thought of Rhodes as her future husband. Her former husband had died, and she saw Rhodes as the logical candidate to replace him. As far as she was concerned, they were the perfect match. So she'd been quite disappointed when Rhodes showed his obtuseness by marrying Ivy Daniel instead of her.

After Rhodes's marriage, Mrs. Wilkie had re-created herself. She'd let her hair, which had been a shocking shade of orange, return to its natural color. She'd gotten a job and begun dressing in very businesslike outfits. Rhodes was no psychologist, but it seemed to him that she was trying to become a lot more like Ivy. She was also trying to let Rhodes know what a big mistake he had made by marrying the wrong woman. In every encounter he had with her, she made it clear that she hadn't given up on him.

Rhodes grimaced at Hack and picked up his extension. The call probably wasn't a coincidence. The job Mrs. Wilkie had gotten was in the office of James Allen.

"This is the sheriff," Rhodes said.

"Sheriff Rhodes?"

Rhodes wondered why people always asked that after he'd just identified himself.

"That's right," he said. He took off his glasses and laid them on the desk. "What can I do for you, Mrs. Wilkie?"

"Mr. Allen was just telling me about Mr. Berry," she said. "I was sorry to hear it. Mr. Berry was a nice man."

Mrs. Wilkie sounded genuinely sad, and Rhodes wondered if she'd developed an interest in Berry.

"Did you know him well?" Rhodes asked.

"No, but I think it was nice that he was interested in the history of the county. Don't you think we should all be interested in history, Sheriff?"

Rhodes agreed that an interest in history was a wonderful thing. He wondered where the conversation was going.

Mrs. Wilkie said, "Mr. Allen said you'd be working hard to find out who killed Mr. Berry."

"That's my job."

"Well, I thought I might be able to help."

"How?" Rhodes asked. "Do you know something about the murder?"

Mrs. Wilkie turned coy. "Not exactly."

Rhodes waited. The silence dragged itself out for several seconds.

"Would you like to come out to the precinct so I can tell you?" Mrs. Wilkie asked.

"I have to follow up on some leads," Rhodes said. He wasn't going to put himself in Mrs. Wilkie's clutches if he could avoid it. "I'll be busy the rest of the day. Do you have something for me?"

"Yes, but I'd prefer to tell you about it in person."

Rhodes knew there was absolutely nothing Mrs. Wilkie could tell him in person that she couldn't tell him over the phone just as well.

"I'm sure you would," he said. "But there's no way I can get out there today, and every minute counts in a murder investigation." Rhodes thought he might be laying it on a little thick, but it was the truth. "Why don't you tell me now? It could be important."

"Oh, all right." Mrs. Wilkie was clearly put out. "I just thought you'd like to know that I heard motorsickles again the other night. I was going to call you then, but I was afraid you'd think I was being silly."

"You didn't see anyone?" Rhodes asked.

"No, I just heard the motorsickles. But they sounded the same way they always do."

Motorcycles all sounded pretty much alike to Rhodes, and he suspected they did to Mrs. Wilkie, too. But he was certain that Mrs. Wilkie had heard two particular motorcycles. He couldn't have said why he was certain, but he was.

"So you don't know where they went," he said.

"No, but they're somewhere around Milsby. I'm sure of that much."

"Thanks, Mrs. Wilkie. I'll check it out this afternoon. You've been a big help, as usual."

"Why, thank you, Sheriff. But I'm just doing my duty as a citizen."

"And I appreciate it. Good-bye, and thanks again."

Rhodes hung up and looked at Hack. The dispatcher

was still smirking. So was Lawton. They looked at each other, smirked some more, and looked back at Rhodes.

"That Miz Wilkie," Hack said. "You got to give her credit for stickin' to a job once she takes it on. Sooner or later, Sheriff, she's gonna marry you, whether you like it or not. You might as well ditch Ivy now and give it up."

"It might not be as easy for her as you think," Rhodes said. "Mrs. McGee might get you first."

He knew it was a low blow, even as he said it. Mrs. McGee was the woman Hack had been seeing for a while, and the dispatcher didn't like talking about her when Lawton was around. Lawton liked to tease him.

Well, if you can dish it out, you have to be able to take it, Rhodes thought.

Lawton didn't miss his cue. He said, "He's right about that, Hack. That Miz McGee's had her cap set for you since she first set eyes on you. You might's well give in and save yourself some trouble."

Hack's face started to turn red, and Rhodes knew he had to change the subject before things got out of hand.

"Mrs. Wilkie said she heard motorcycles out at Milsby," he said.

Hack turned toward him, and the red started to fade from his face.

"You think it's those two gangsters back again?" he asked.

"Could be," Rhodes said, though *gangsters* wasn't exactly the word he would have chosen to describe the two men he was thinking of. "They seem to have a way of turning up when things get bad around here."

"Looks like they'd have learned their lesson by now," Lawton said.

"Some people never learn," Hack said, giving Lawton a hard look.

"Especially those two," Rhodes said, before the conversation could get sidetracked.

"I was hopin' they might die," Hack said. "I guess they're just too mean."

"That's probably it," Rhodes said.

The two men they were talking about were called Rapper and Nellie. They were supposedly members of a motorcycle gang called Los Muertos, though no other members of the gang had ever showed up in Blacklin County.

In their first encounter with Rhodes, Rapper had lost the ends of a couple of fingers. That had been enough to keep him away for a while.

In the next confrontation, Nellie and Rapper had both ended up in the hospital, Nellie with two broken ribs and Rapper with a severe wound in his thigh, where Rhodes had stuck a hay hook. They'd sneaked away from the hospital because they'd thought they might be charged with murder.

"Broken ribs never killed anybody," Lawton said. "But I'll bet that Rapper fella is still walkin' funny."

Rhodes hoped so. He'd used the hay hook on Rapper because Rapper had been trying to kill him.

"Maybe they knew a doctor somewhere else," Rhodes said.

"What do you reckon they're up to?" Hack asked. "You think they've got somethin' to do with this cemetery business?"

"I wouldn't be a bit surprised," Rhodes said.

EIGHT

BEFORE RHODES LEFT the jail, he asked about the ghost again. "Not a peep out of him today," Lawton said. "Maybe he's moved on to haunt somebody else. That'd be fine with me. I'm tired of ghosts. I'm ready for things to get back to normal around here."

"Things ain't never been normal around here," Hack said.

"You got that right," Lawton said, being more agreeable than usual.

"What about Ty Berry?" Hack asked Rhodes. "You really got some investigatin' to do this afternoon, or were you just puttin' Miz Wilkie off?"

"I thought I might have a talk with some of the cemetery association presidents," Rhodes said. "And maybe some of the Sons and Daughters of Texas, see if they have an idea what Ty's been up to and whether he's tangled with anybody lately. While I'm doing that, give Ruth Grady a call. If she's got the situation with those goats straightened out, have her and Buddy Reynolds go out to the cemetery and impound Ty Berry's pickup. She can bring it in and go over it for evidence."

"You think she'll find anything?" Hack asked.

"I doubt it. I've already searched it. I probably messed it up a little."

"Ruth won't like that."

Rhodes agreed that she wouldn't. Ruth was a stickler for doing things the right way. But Rhodes had wanted to know what was in the cab of the pickup, and he hadn't wanted to wait.

"Tell Buddy to go around to all the houses around the cemetery and ask if anyone heard shots last night," Rhodes said.

Buddy was another of the deputies. He had a mild puritanical streak, but he could be counted on to ask the question in a way that wouldn't scare everyone half to death.

"Hard to hear a little old .22 from any distance," Hack said.

"Not if it was a still night," Lawton said. "You can hear things for miles up on that hill."

"It wasn't still last night," Hack pointed out. "The wind was blowing up a storm."

"Didn't say it *was* still," Lawton said. "Just said you could hear a .22 a long way *if* it was."

"Never mind that," Rhodes said, heading off the argument. "Just tell Buddy to ask around. I'll go to see the presidents of the associations."

"What about Faye Knape?" Hack asked. "You gonna talk to her, too?"

"I guess so. She might not be much help, though."

"What you need to do is find out who's been taking that stuff from the cemeteries," Lawton said. "That's who killed Berry, I'll bet."

"Anything's possible right now," Rhodes said. "But I have to start somewhere, and I can't talk to the people who've been stealing from the cemeteries because I can't find them. I've been trying for weeks, and I haven't had much luck."

"Maybe today will be the day things turn around," Hack said.

Rhodes hoped he was right.

FOR MOST OF THE REST of the afternoon, it looked as if Hack had been wrong. Rhodes talked to the presidents of five cemetery associations, all of whom were genuinely sorry about what had happened to Berry but none of whom had really talked to him within the past week.

And none of them had actually done what they'd said about patrolling their own cemeteries, either. It had been too wet or too cold or too this or too that for them to do what they'd talked about. What it all added up to was that they weren't nearly as enthusiastic about the possibility of confronting the looters as Berry had been.

Frank Conners was in charge of the Sealy Cemetery. He operated a feed store, and he and Rhodes stood out in front while they talked. Rhodes could smell the rich odor of cottonseed meal coming from five dusty sacks of it that were stacked against the wall.

Conners said, "That little cemetery is a long way off the main road, and I got to thinking what I'd do if I caught anybody there in the middle of the night. Sure, I could call your office on my cell phone, but what if they saw me? What if they decided to do something about me? I'm licensed to carry a concealed handgun, but I'm not sure I could actually shoot it at anybody. I'd most likely just wind up getting killed."

All the private cemeteries were located in out-of-the-way places, off the main roads. Some of them could be reached only by one-lane dirt roads that hardly anyone ever traveled. They had been started long ago, in the nineteenth century in some cases, by families too far from town to consider traveling there to bury relatives, or by small rural churches whose congregations had long ago moved away or died, or by small communities of which nothing now remained other than the graves of the former residents.

People wanted to keep the cemeteries in appropriate condition and they wanted the remains of the people buried there to stay exactly where they were. The current caretakers would never have considered moving the graves to a more accessible location. Rhodes didn't blame them, but the remote locations were what made it so easy for someone to loot the graveyards, what made it so hard for Rhodes's department to patrol them, and what made it so dangerous for anyone to try to protect them from looters. Though, come to think of it, being right there in the city limits hadn't helped Ty Berry even a little bit.

"I did drive by the place at night a time or two," Conners told Rhodes. "But I never saw anything. Tell you the truth, Sheriff, I can understand why you haven't caught anybody yet. And with what happened to Ty, I don't think anybody'll be going out there at night to help you. I don't envy you your job."

Rhodes was glad for the understanding, but it was no more help to him than what he'd heard from other association presidents. He was beginning to think he wasn't going to find out anything at all.

But then he went to talk to Faye Knape.

FAYE KNAPE LIVED in an old frame house near the downtown area. It was late afternoon when Rhodes arrived. It would have been near sundown if there had been any sun. The thick clouds made it seem almost like night, and the tall pecan trees in the yard made things even darker. There was a light shining through the front windows, however, and Rhodes could see cats sitting in some of them. Rhodes did a quick count and came up with three. He knew there were probably more than that, though not many more. Maybe six or eight altogether, though

Rhodes wasn't sure how many cats Mrs. Knape had. He didn't know whether even Mrs. Knape was sure.

Mrs. Knape's husband had died of colon cancer some years before, and she'd transferred all her affection to her cats. Her love for the animals was well-known in Clearview. She had all colors: white, black, black and white, gray, orange, and calico. Rhodes, who was slightly allergic to cats, hoped he'd be able to keep himself from sneezing while he was in the house, but he knew it was a vain hope.

He stepped up on the porch and knocked on the door. At the first hollow tap, all the cats disappeared from the windows as if they'd never been there.

After a few seconds Rhodes could hear someone inside. The porch light came on, and Mrs. Knape peered out at him through one of the small glass panes set in the upper part of the door. When she saw Rhodes, she threw a deadbolt, snapped a lock, and opened the door.

"Good evening, Sheriff," she said. "I suppose you're here about Ty Berry."

She was a tall woman, nearly as tall as Rhodes. Even taller if you took into account her masses of amazingly black hair. The hair color would have been even more amazing had it been real, which it wasn't. Mrs. Knape was well over sixty, and she'd been dyeing her hair for years. She did it herself, and she used Clairol Nice 'n' Easy, according to Ivy, who'd seen her buying it at Wal-Mart.

Rhodes wasn't at all shocked to hear Mrs. Knape knew about Ty Berry, since everyone else did.

"That's why I'm here," he said.

"Well, you might as well come inside. I'll tell you everything I know."

Rhodes wondered just how much that would be as she

ushered him into a hallway, where his rubber-soled shoes made squeaking noises on the hardwood floor. After only a few steps, they turned right, into the living room. It was an old-fashioned room that fit perfectly with the house's exterior. It held a black upright piano, a Duncan Phyfe coffee table, an overstuffed sofa, and an armchair to match. The armchair had an antimacassar on the back. On the end table by the chair there was a thick black Bible, beside which sat a box of tissues and a heavy cut-glass vase filled with dried wildflowers. The room's wallpaper had a busy floral pattern.

Rhodes could smell the sharp ammoniac odor of cat boxes. He couldn't smell the cats themselves, and he couldn't see them. He couldn't see the boxes, either, and he assumed they were in another part of the house.

"Where are the cats?" he asked, and then he sneezed.

"Bless you," Mrs. Knape said. "Help yourself to a tissue."

"Thanks," Rhodes said, plucking one from the box.

"The boys don't like strangers," Mrs. Knape told him. "They've all gone into hiding. They're probably all under my bed or in one of the closets."

"They're shy?" Rhodes said.

"Oh, yes. They're very shy until they get to know you. Have a seat."

Rhodes sat in the armchair. It wasn't that he disliked cats, but he was just as glad that the "boys" wouldn't be sitting in on the conversation. He thought he could detect an itchiness beginning in the corner of his left eye, which was probably already turning red.

Mrs. Knape sat on the sofa. "Now," she said. "About Ty Berry."

"What about him?" Rhodes asked, resisting the urge

to rub his eyes. Rubbing would only make things worse, as he knew from experience.

Mrs. Knape leaned forward confidentially. "I'm sure he was behind the whole thing."

Rhodes wasn't sure exactly what whole thing she was talking about. So he took a wild guess.

"Do you mean you think he killed himself?"

"Of course. That would be just like him. After he'd taken everything he could from the cemeteries, what else could he do? He knew you'd catch up to him sooner or later, so he took the only way out that was left to him. The poor man."

She said the last words without the least trace of sympathy as far as Rhodes could tell. Or irony, for that matter. She seemed so satisfied with her version of events that Rhodes almost hated to spoil her evening for her. But he figured he had to. It was his job.

First he had to sneeze, however. When he was finished with that, he said, "Ty Berry didn't kill himself."

"How do you know that?"

"There was no weapon near his body. Or anywhere else around."

"Well, of course there wouldn't be a weapon. He probably disposed of it."

"Before or after he killed himself?"

Mrs. Knape sat up straight, her spine stiff as an ironing board.

"There's no need for sarcasm, Sheriff."

Rhodes apologized. He didn't generally resort to sarcasm. He told himself that it was the itching in his eyes that made him do it.

"Anyway," Mrs. Knape said, "he was a clever man. I'm sure he could have found a way to get rid of the weapon."

Rhodes decided he wouldn't argue. He knew it wouldn't do any good.

"Let's say he did commit suicide," Rhodes said. "How can we prove that he was stealing the things from the cemeteries?"

"Oh, that," Mrs. Knape said with a small, satisfied smile. "Why, that's the easy part."

NINE

WHAT FAYE KNAPE purported to know was that Ty Berry had been, as she put it, "in cahoots with" an antique dealer named Richard Rascoe. The two of them were using Rascoe's store to "fence the goods."

Rhodes thought she might have been watching a few too many old cop movies on television, though he didn't say so. Instead he told her that though the name sounded vaguely familiar, he didn't think he'd ever met Richard Rascoe.

"That's because you're not an antique collector," Mrs. Knape said.

Rhodes said that she was right about that. He didn't have much time for hobbies, though he did like to watch old movies when he had the time. Which wasn't often.

"If you collected antiques," she told him, "you'd know all about Richard Rascoe. He has a store in Thurston, and he's been written up in the newspaper."

Rhodes sneezed, wiped his nose with a tissue, and remembered then where he'd heard Rascoe's name. It had been several months earlier. Ivy had told him about the new store that was opening down in Thurston, a little town in the southern part of the county.

There was even less left of Thurston than there was of Clearview, and some of the local citizens had gotten the idea that one way to bring some business back to town might be to fix up some of the old buildings and rent them out, dirt cheap, as antique stores. A lot of small Texas towns on or near highways had made similar efforts, and some of those efforts had actually paid off. Rhodes wondered why Clearview didn't try something like that before the rest of the downtown buildings collapsed.

While Rhodes hadn't noticed any special growth boom in Thurston the last time he'd been through there, the refurbished buildings did look good, and there were at least two or three cars parked along the street, maybe in front of Rascoe's store, though Rhodes hadn't paid it any special attention.

"So you think this Rascoe and Ty Berry were engaged in the illegal sale of cemetery artifacts," Rhodes said.

"That's right," Mrs. Knape said. "There's not any doubt about it. I saw some of the goods right there in Mr. Rascoe's store."

"Why didn't you call?" Rhodes asked, just before he sneezed again.

"Bless you. I was going to call. But I wanted to go back one more time and have another look just to make sure."

"And you haven't gone yet?"

"No. I was planning to go tomorrow. But I'm sure I'm right. There's really no question about it."

It didn't seem likely to Rhodes that anyone would be stupid enough to display items from local cemeteries in a store that was practically sitting by the highway.

"How did you identify the items?" he asked.

"Oh, it was easy. There's an angel there from the Kennedy Cemetery. I knew it immediately."

"How?"

"Why, Kennedy's my maiden name. My father and mother are both buried in the Kennedy Cemetery. I visit their graves at least once a week, and I've seen everything in the cemetery many times."

She sounded convincing. Rhodes thought it would be a good idea to have a talk with Rascoe, though he still believed it was stupid to be displaying something stolen from a cemetery not more than fifteen miles away. Rascoe must have known someone would recognize it. He said as much to Mrs. Knape.

"I'm sure he knew," she said. "But he didn't really intend for anyone to see the angel. It was in a back room that had a little sign saying 'Employees Only' on the door."

Rhodes couldn't resist asking why she'd gone through the door.

She wasn't the least abashed by his question. "Those little back rooms are where dealers always keep some of their best things, the kind of things they're saving for their big-city clients who drive from Dallas or Houston. Naturally I wasn't going to let a little thing like a sign keep me from looking in that room."

Rhodes said he wasn't aware that she was a collector.

"I collect china and glassware," she said. "I have some wonderful R.S. Prussia pieces in the dining room. I'd be glad to show you if you'd like to see them."

Rhodes said that he might like to see them some other time and asked if she would be willing to identify the angel.

"Of course. We can't let Ty Berry and Richard Rascoe get away with their little scam any longer."

"There's just one more thing," Rhodes said. "Assuming that the angel is from the Kennedy Cemetery, you haven't told me how I'm supposed to prove that Rascoe got it from Ty Berry."

Mrs. Knape looked shocked that Rhodes could make such a ridiculous statement.

"Where else would he have gotten it?" she asked, as if that settled the matter for good and all.

"From whoever took it. I don't see any proof that it was Berry."

"Well," Mrs. Knape said. "I never. Being called a liar is very insulting, Sheriff."

"I didn't say you were a liar. I just said that there was nothing to connect Berry to the angel."

"Well, I'm sure there is. Since he's the one who stole it, there's no question that the proof is there. You're the sheriff, so it's up to you to find the connection."

"If there is one," Rhodes said.

Mrs. Knape's face was getting red. "There is one. I know there is. And you'd better find it. I have a lot of friends in this county, Sheriff, and we'll remember this at the next election."

There it was, Rhodes thought, everyone's favorite threat: do what we want, or we'll vote you out of office. Unfortunately, what people wanted didn't always fit the facts. He was willing to believe that Rascoe had the angel in his store, but he didn't think Berry had anything to do with its being there. Berry had been entirely too vehement about protection for the cemeteries to have participated in any looting. And he certainly hadn't killed himself, not unless someone had taken the pistol away.

Rhodes thought about that for a second. It was actually possible, if not likely, that something like that could have happened. Berry could have shot himself at the edge of the grave, dropped the pistol, and fallen in. Someone could have picked up the gun and removed it from the scene.

But Rhodes had never heard of a suicide shooting himself in the middle of the forehead. Again, it was possible.

But it was unlikely in the extreme, no matter what Mrs. Knape might like to think.

"I'll do what I can," he told her. "But I can't promise things will work out the way you want them to."

"It's not that I want them to work out any certain way," she said. "That's just the way they are."

"We'll see," Rhodes said.

He stood up, and Mrs. Knape walked him to the door. As soon as he was outside, he started rubbing his eyes.

TEN

RHODES DROVE INTO his dark driveway, checked to make sure Ivy had fed Speedo, and went inside. The clothes dryer was humming, so Ivy must have put his wash in it.

Yancey bounded up to Rhodes, yipping excitedly, which was the way he always yipped.

"You're thrilled to see me, right?" Rhodes said.

Yancey responded by trying to bite Rhodes's ankles.

Ivy came through the door. "I'm thrilled to see you, too, but I'm not trying to bite you."

Ivy had brown eyes and short, graying hair that hadn't been touched up with Clairol Nice 'n' Easy.

"You can do that later," Rhodes said. "Unless there's a really good movie on."

Yancey stopped barking and looked alertly from one of them to the other.

"You shouldn't talk like that in front of the dog," Ivy said.

"He can move out if he's embarrassed."

"Do you think Speedo would be willing to share his igloo?"

Rhodes said he didn't think so and asked about supper.

"I have a really good plan for that," Ivy said.

"And what would that be?"

She smiled. "You're taking me out."

THE ROUND-UP RESTAURANT was located about a half mile out of town, just down the highway from the Wal-

Mart, which was no coincidence. Everything was migrating in that direction, Rhodes thought, including the town's largest car dealership, which had set up a huge new lot and showroom nearby.

The Round-Up didn't cater to people with elevated cholesterol levels or highly refined tastes. There was a portable sign out front, lit from within to proclaim that

ABSOLUTELY NO CHICKEN
FISH
OR VEGETARIAN DISHES
CAN BE FOUND
ON OUR MENU!

There was, however, a section of the restaurant reserved for nonsmokers, but only because the manager had been told that such an area was required by a city ordinance.

It wasn't a place where Rhodes ate often. It didn't fit in with the low-fat regime instituted by Ivy. In fact, he'd been there only once before, a day or so after the place had opened. But he'd been looking forward to a return trip.

He pulled his red and white 1959 Edsel Citation four-door hardtop into a parking lot that was crowded with pickups and SUVs. He found a spot beside a Chevy Blazer with a bumper sticker that read

Jesus loves you!
(Everyone else thinks you're an asshole.)

"I wonder how whoever owns that car knew I was going to be here tonight?" Rhodes said.

"You shouldn't take it so personally," Ivy told him. "It could be just an expression of religious freedom."

"Right," Rhodes said, getting out of the Edsel.

Like Yancey and Speedo, the car had been acquired during the course of an investigation. Rhodes had never even thought about buying an Edsel until he saw it. Then he couldn't resist. And besides, it was cheap.

Some people thought the Edsel was one of the ugliest cars ever built. Not Rhodes. He liked the squared-off roof, the horse-collar grille, and the sculptured sheet-metal body. He even liked the widely despised drum speedometer and the push-button transmission with the buttons in the center of the steering wheel.

Ivy was less enthusiastic, but at least she never complained about riding in it.

They went inside the restaurant, a sprawling building of rough wood with high ceilings and rafters lined with antlers of all sizes, hundreds of pairs of them. Rhodes wasn't quite sure what the antlers had to do with anything, since venison wasn't on the menu. He supposed they were part of the rustic decorations, which also consisted of old metal signs advertising things like Grapette soda, Sinclair gasoline, and Hadacol.

The large room was noisy with the sounds of talking and the music of the jukebox, which was stocked with country music from an era when the sound was actually "country." Rhodes recognized the voice of Jim Reeves, singing something about pride going before a fall.

A waiter led Rhodes and Ivy to a table in the non-smoking section. Several people greeted them as they made their way through the tables, shaking hands with Rhodes and asking how the sheriff business was. No one had the bad taste to ask about Ty Berry.

The waiter handed them menus when they were seated. Rhodes didn't need the menu. He already knew what he wanted: the item billed as "The World's Biggest Chicken-Fried Steak."

Although the steak was indeed enormous, Rhodes wasn't sure the claim was true. He'd been in at least four different restaurants that all professed to sell "The World's Biggest Chicken-Fried Steak." He'd never measured them, and he didn't know anyone who had. All he knew for sure was that the one served in the Round-Up was awfully big.

It was so large, in fact, that the edges dangled over the sides of the plate. The potatoes that came with it, mashed with the skins still on them, had to be served in a separate dish.

Both steak and potatoes were smothered in thick white gravy with flecks of black pepper scattered throughout. It was almost as good as a hot roast beef sandwich. Maybe better. He even ordered a Dr Pepper to go along with his meal.

Ivy was much more restrained than Rhodes. She ordered a small filet and a salad. Rhodes was a little surprised that the Round-Up deigned to serve salads, but he supposed that there had to be some concessions made just in case there was someone who was so unenlightened as to want to order something other than meat.

While they waited for Ivy's salad to arrive, they talked about their day. Ivy worked at an insurance office, where it just so happened that Ty Berry had a life insurance policy. Naturally the news of his death had been big news there.

"Any leads?" she asked.

Rhodes didn't mind talking about it in a public place, at least not in the Round-Up, mainly because he was sure that no one could hear him more than six inches away, thanks to all the noise, part of which was being currently

made by Hank Snow, who was on the jukebox explaining
to a truck driver that he'd been everywhere.

"Not much," Rhodes said, telling Ivy what he knew
and ending with his visit to Faye Knape.

The salad arrived. Ivy took a bite and said, "Faye and
her cats. I thought your eyes looked a little red."

"I rubbed them," Rhodes confessed. "I couldn't help
myself."

"I like cats," Ivy said. "It's too bad you're allergic
to them. We could get us a couple if you weren't."

"I like cats, too. But I don't think Speedo and Yancey
would want to share the house with them."

"Cats don't share," Ivy said. "They take over. But
I've gotten you off the subject of your investigation.
What did Faye have to tell you?"

Rhodes went on to explain Mrs. Knape's theory of how
Ty Berry had died.

Ivy's eyes widened. "Suicide? Really?"

"That's what she says."

"I'll have to get Mr. Tacker to talk to her," Ivy said.
Tacker was the owner of the insurance agency. "He can
save the company money if that's the case."

"It's not the case," Rhodes said, and told her why.

"Oh," Ivy said.

She finished her salad as Rhodes told her about the
angel and about Mrs. Knape's theory that Berry had arranged with Richard Rascoe for its sale.

Ivy wiped her mouth with her napkin. "That doesn't
sound very smart."

"It wouldn't be," Rhodes said. "And there's no proof
at all of a connection between Berry and the angel."

Their steaks arrived then, and Rhodes got ready for
some serious eating. In addition to the steak and potatoes,
there was a basket of large, soft whole wheat rolls and a

dish of real butter. It was almost enough to make eating low-fat veggie bologna for lunch worthwhile.

When they were done, Rhodes was completely satisfied. There was even a bite or two of steak left on his plate, so he felt highly self-righteous. He was about to ask Ivy if she knew of any great historical events that had occurred in A.D. 11, but he didn't get a chance. The waiter came to their table and said that there was a phone call for him.

"It's Mr. Jensen at the jail," the waiter said.

Rhodes had let Hack know where he'd be going, as he always did. There was no way of knowing what emergencies might come up at any given moment.

He followed the waiter to the telephone at the checkout counter. After Hank Locklin had finished begging someone to send him the pillow that she dreamed on, Rhodes picked up the receiver.

"This is Rhodes," he said.

"You gotta come to the jail," Hack said. "The ghost's got loose."

"Loose?" Rhodes said.

"Loose, out on the town, runnin' wild. Are you comin' or not?"

"I'll be there in ten minutes," Rhodes said.

ELEVEN

IVY WENT TO THE JAIL with Rhodes. She said that there wasn't anything good on TV that evening and that whatever had Hack so excited would probably be more entertaining than TV anyway.

When they got there, they found four Clearview teenagers, two boys and two girls, who were in a highly agitated state, to put it mildly. They were all gathered around Hack, and they were talking at once.

Hack looked up when Rhodes and Ivy came through the door. The relief on his face was obvious.

"Here's the sheriff," he said. "You can tell him all about it."

The four young people turned from Hack and started for Rhodes. Ivy grinned and went over to talk to Hack while Rhodes dealt with the situation.

He sat at his desk and held up his hands. "First of all," he said, "let me get your names."

He got out a report form and took down the names: Jennifer Colton, Lisa Wetmore, Jason Crites, and Larry Lake. Then he elected Jason the spokesman. Jason was thin and blond and had several dots of something that looked suspiciously like Clearasil on his chin.

"Now," Rhodes said. "Tell me what happened."

"Well, we were riding around," Jason said, "and Jennifer's, like, 'Let's go to the graveyard,' but I go, 'Isn't it against the law to drive around there at night?' and she goes, 'I don't think so,' and then Lisa goes—"

Jennifer, a small brunette who probably didn't weigh

more than ninety pounds, interrupted him. "I didn't say it wasn't against the law, Sheriff."

Lisa, who wasn't much bigger but who had very blond hair and big, wide eyes said, "You did so say it wasn't against the law, and anyway, it's all Jason's fault because that old car of his has a loose battery cable, and if he hadn't been driving so fast it wouldn't have come off when we hit that bump and then we wouldn't be here in the first place and—"

Rhodes held up a hand to stop her. "Just hold on a minute. Jason's telling this. I'll get your side of the story when he's finished."

"That's not fair, Sheriff," Larry Lake said. He was short and had a determined look. "You ought to listen to Lisa because she's the one that nearly got killed by the ghost before it got after all of us and she's the one that tried to tell Jason that somebody'd been buried out there today, which if Jason had listened to her, he never would've—"

Rhodes held up his hand again. He was beginning to see why there had been a note of near-panic in Hack's voice during the phone call he'd made to the Round-Up. When Rhodes had been a youngster, he and most of his friends would have been paralyzed into speechlessness in the presence of a sheriff or any other representative of the power of the law. Now kids felt no need to defer to anyone. He was sure the four in front of him would have been just as voluble if he'd been the governor or the president. He couldn't make up his mind about whether that was good or bad.

He glanced over in the dispatcher's direction. Both Ivy and Hack were watching him and grinning broadly.

"Look," Rhodes said to the teenagers. "You're going to have to let one person tell the story. Then, when it's done, the rest of you can tell me anything that's been left out. Until then, just keep quiet.''

They looked at him as if he were some kind of relic of the Stone Age, which he probably was. But at least they let Jason get on with it and tell his tale.

It seemed that, over Lisa's objections, they had decided to take a drive through the cemetery. Sure, there had been a funeral there that afternoon, but they weren't planning to do anything disrespectful.

Rhodes was pretty sure they'd been planning to park for a while in the peaceful darkness, but Jason didn't say so, and Rhodes let it go.

They'd driven around for a few minutes, and Lisa had seen something that scared her. It hadn't been too far from the mound of dirt that covered Mr. McCoy. She'd screamed, Jason had sped up, and the car had hit a bump.

''That's when the bad stuff started,'' Jason said. ''The battery cable came off, and the car died, and we're all, like, 'What're we gonna do now?' ''

''Open the hood and connect the battery cable,'' Rhodes suggested.

Jason looked at him with disgust. ''Oh, sure, like we didn't think of that. But the little dealy-bopper that pops the hood is broken and we couldn't get the hood open to get to the battery. So Lisa's in the back seat, freaking out and going, 'It's a ghost! It's a ghost! Get us out of here! Get us out of here!' and I'm, like, 'There's nothing I can do.' So Larry and I decided we'd have to walk to my house and get some tools, like maybe a screwdriver or a pair of pliers, and open the hood that way if we could.''

''Why didn't you call your parents?'' Rhodes asked, figuring that at least one of them, if not all of them, had a cell phone.

The faintest tinge of red crept into Jason's face. ''It

was, like, we thought that might not be a good idea, you know? I mean, we weren't really supposed to be there and all, so we thought we could just go get some tools and open the hood and fix things up. We didn't really think there was a ghost or anything.''

"But you saw one," Rhodes said.

"No, we never did. It was Lisa that saw it."

Lisa spoke up. "Two. I saw two."

"Okay, two," Jason said. "Anyway, me and Larry told the girls that we'd all have to walk. Jennifer didn't mind, but Lisa goes, 'I'm not gonna get out of this car, not if you try to drag me out with a chain.' She said we could leave, but she was staying and we'd just have to lock the doors real good and she'd scrunch down in the floor.

"So that's what we did. We got out and pushed all the door locks down and left her there. It was like really dark, but we had a flashlight so we could see where we were going. I guess we were about to the cemetery gate when she passed us.''

"Passed you?" Rhodes said. "In the car?"

"No, she was running. She must've been doing sixty, easy. I looked at Larry and I'm, like 'Was that the ghost?' and he goes, 'No, that was Lisa.' We followed her all the way here and we were running, too, since we thought whatever was after her might be after us, but we never caught her."

Rhodes looked over at Hack.

"That's right," Hack said. "She busted through the front door pantin' like a dog. She must've run all the way here. The others were a little ways behind her."

"Me and Jason could've caught her," Larry said defensively, as if he didn't want the word to get around that he'd been outrun by a girl. "We just didn't want to go off and leave Jennifer by herself."

"I can see that," Rhodes said. "What happened to make you run, Lisa?"

"It was the ghosts," she said. "I heard something behind the car, some kind of horrible noise like maybe some old man trying to grunt like a pig, and I got up and looked out the back window and there they were, right out there in the road. And I'm, like, 'I'm not gonna stay in here and let them get me,' so I unlocked the door and jumped out and ran."

"What did they look like?" Rhodes asked.

"They were awful! Shiny and black with their hair parted in the middle like in the olden days, and they were running after me."

"Did you see them behind you?" Rhodes asked.

"Well, no, but I didn't have to see them to know they were back there, did I? I mean, they were right out there in the road, so they must've been after me."

"All right," Rhodes said. "Anything else?"

None of them could think of anything, so Rhodes had Hack get on the radio and call for a deputy to come get them and take them home.

"What about the ghosts?" Lisa wanted to know.

"That's something I want to see for myself," Rhodes said.

"What about my car?" Jason asked.

"You can pick it up tomorrow."

"My dad's really not gonna like that."

"I don't blame him," Rhodes said.

THE RAIN HAD been over for hours, but the clouds had hung around, making the night very dark. Rhodes put the Edsel in the garage and walked Ivy to the door.

"I don't see why I can't go with you," she said.

"Official business. I don't want to put a civilian in harm's way."

"Baloney," Ivy said. "You know there's no such thing as ghosts."

"Try telling that to Lisa," Rhodes said.

Ivy laughed. "I don't think I could get a word in edgewise with anybody in that bunch. You looked a little harassed, yourself."

"Maybe I'm getting too old to deal with the younger members of the public."

"I don't think so. Anyway, even if I could get a word in edgewise, I'm not sure I could convince her. She must have seen *something* out there."

"You couldn't convince our prisoners, either," Rhodes said. "They think there's a ghost in the jail. So I'm kind of glad to hear about these other two."

"Why?" Ivy asked.

"Because now either the whole town's infested, or else the one in the jail's found a partner and left."

"What if the whole town's infested?" Ivy wanted to know. "Who you gonna call? Ghostbusters?"

"Nope," Rhodes said. "I don't think they have a Clearview branch."

"So it's all up to you, then."

"Yeah. I hope I don't get slimed."

"So do I," Ivy said.

TWELVE

THE WIND WAS BLOWING the cedars around, and the oak trees were thrashing. But the wind hadn't blown the clouds away, and the cemetery was dark as the graves that filled it.

Rhodes drove to the McCoy plot. Jason's car, a ten-year-old Chevrolet Lumina, sat in the road nearby. There was nothing else around it. Rhodes shone his spotlight on the car and then on the mound of earth that covered McCoy's last resting place. The soil shone wet and black under the light, but it didn't appear that Mr. McCoy had disturbed it. For that matter, it didn't seem to have been disturbed by anyone or anything.

Rhodes thought of the two figures he'd seen running across the clearing that afternoon in the rain. Maybe some homeless people were camping in the woods down there, though he'd seen no sign of them when he searched. If they were there, though, they might have thought it would be funny to scare someone who was driving through the cemetery. Just why anyone would think that was funny, Rhodes couldn't say. But if he'd learned anything in his career, it was that you could never tell what someone might do for a laugh.

Or maybe they'd been the monument thieves.

Rhodes got out of the car and used his flashlight to have a look around. He didn't find anything suspicious. Clyde Ballinger and his crew had cleaned up around the grave site. The canopy was gone, along with the folding chairs and the fake grass. The only things left were a couple of flower arrangements and some random white petals on the ground.

The night air was damp and cool, and it settled on Rhodes like a shroud. He got back in the car and toured the whole cemetery. There was nothing alive there, not that he could see. If he hadn't seen those running figures in the clearing earlier in the afternoon, he would have been tempted to dismiss the teens' story out of hand.

As it was, he didn't. They might very well have seen someone. He just didn't know who.

Or what. For all he knew, there really were ghosts out there. It was certainly the right kind of night for them.

After a little more than half an hour, Rhodes still hadn't spotted anyone or anything. No one else had driven through the cemetery gates or even passed by on the street, so Rhodes decided to go back to the jail.

He was about to head for the gates when he thought he saw something move out of the corner of his eye. He stopped the car, got out, and turned his flashlight in the direction of the motion. The beam showed only immobile stones, but down at the bottom of the hill, a dark and shapeless shadow darted between a couple of sooty monuments topped respectively by a soldier and an angel with widespread wings. The shadow was moving faster than any human being could possibly run, Rhodes thought.

Rhodes yelled, "Hey!" but got no response, so he began to run down the hill, dodging trees and the larger tombstones and hurtling over the smaller ones, his shoes squishing into the wet ground when his feet landed and sucking out when he picked them up.

Even with the bad footing, he was moving awfully fast, thanks more to the slope and to gravity than to any natural athletic ability. But for just a moment, he felt almost like "Will-o'-the-wisp" Dan Rhodes, who'd returned the opening kickoff of the football season for a touchdown.

But it was only for a moment. He'd almost reached the bottom of the hill when he was distracted by the whooshing sound of wings over his head. He glanced up, caught a quick glimpse of what he thought was most likely an owl, and the toe of his shoe caught on the top edge of a stone. The next thing he knew, he was flying through the air, though not exactly with the greatest of ease.

He didn't have much time to be uneasy, however, because he hit the wet ground in full stretch. The flashlight flew out of his hand, and he slid forward for several feet before coming to a stop when his head connected with a tombstone. The blow sent a sharp pain down his spine and made his skull feel like an egg that had been cracked against the edge of a cast-iron frying pan. Little lights sparkled in front of his eyes.

He turned over on his back and lay there for a while, thinking that he was too old to be jumping tombstones, even low ones, and that he'd gotten what he deserved.

Or maybe he hadn't. Maybe there was more to come. Maybe the ghost or ghoul or whatever was roaming around the cemetery at night would come along and do to him whatever it was that ghosts and ghouls did.

What did they do, anyway? Rhodes couldn't think of anything.

But if they didn't do anything, why were people afraid of them?

He couldn't answer that question, either, and he realized that his mind was rambling. He shook his head to clear it and wished he hadn't. Now he knew how Humpty-Dumpty felt.

He sat up and looked around for the flashlight. It was

lying about ten feet away, its beam shining along the ground and revealing nothing at all.

He took a deep breath and stood up, putting his hand on top of his head to see if there was any bleeding and also to make sure nothing fell off.

Nothing did, and there was no bleeding, though he could feel the beginnings of a lump. He retrieved his flashlight and pointed it toward the bottom of the hill.

There was nothing there, not that he could see. The question was, should he go down and investigate with his head hurting the way it was?

Of course he should. He was the sheriff, after all. He took another deep breath and walked down the hill.

When he got to the bottom, though his head was still hurting, it had stopped throbbing, and he could think about as clearly as he ever could. He shined the flashlight all around the fence, looking for footprints, though of course ghosts wouldn't leave any.

Ghosts wouldn't need a gap in the fence to get away, either, but that's what Rhodes found, a place near one of the fence posts where two strands of wire had snapped, leaving a gap that even he could slip through with ease. It would have posed no problem at all for a ghost.

The only things past the fence were the woods and the railroad tracks, and Rhodes had already searched that area once that day. He didn't see any point in doing it again, considering that he hadn't found anything the first time. Besides, as fast as the ghost had been moving, it could easily have been in the next county by now.

Rhodes shone his light out at the trees and saw nothing unusual. He stood there for a minute, waiting for something to happen. He didn't know what he was waiting for exactly, maybe for the mournful and far-off howl of a dog.

There was nothing, so Rhodes turned and walked back up the hill to the county car. What he needed was a Dr Pepper and some dry clothes. In that order.

He was driving through the cemetery gates when Hack got him on the radio.

"Just got a call from your friend Miz Wilkie," Hack said.

"What did she have to say?" Rhodes asked.

"'Motorsickles,'" Hack told him.

"I think you've given me that answer before," Rhodes said.

"Déjà vu," Hack said. "That's what they call it when that happens."

"Just what I needed to know," Rhodes said.

THIRTEEN

MILSBY HAD ONCE BEEN a more or less thriving little farm community, not far from Clearview. But the cotton farmers who had supported it had long since died or given up trying to make a living from the land and moved away. The old cotton gin was still there, though it was beginning to collapse inward upon itself from years of neglect.

There were still a few houses around Milsby, and people still lived in them. One of those people was Mrs. Wilkie, and she was waiting for Rhodes's knock on her door.

"Are you all right?" she said, peering at him through the screen.

"I'm fine," Rhodes said. "Just a little tussle with some ghosts."

"Ghosts?"

"Never mind. Hack said you called in to report some motorcycles."

"That's right. I heard them again."

The porch light made Mrs. Wilkie's face look old and drawn. Rhodes wondered for a second what he looked like but decided he didn't want to know. Judging from Mrs. Wilkie's reaction on seeing him, the answer couldn't be good.

"Where were they?" he asked.

"They went right past the house," she said. "Why do they always come back here?"

Rhodes couldn't tell her. He couldn't figure it out, himself. If it was indeed Rapper and Nellie she'd heard, they never seemed to learn a thing from their experiences. He would have thought they'd set up in some other part of the county. But no. Here they were again.

Or maybe not. There was nothing to prove it had been them that Mrs. Wilkie had heard.

"I'll have a look around," Rhodes said. "I appreciate the call."

Mrs. Wilkie smiled. "Would you like to come in for a cup of coffee?"

Rhodes didn't drink coffee, not that he would have accepted the invitation even if he had. He said, "I'd better go look for those motorcycles."

Mrs. Wilkie said that she understood. "I hope you find them."

"Me, too," Rhodes said, though he really wasn't so sure. His previous encounters with Rapper hadn't ended very well for either of them.

RHODES DROVE AROUND the Milsby area for a while, trying to remember which of the old farmhouses might be vacant but still in more or less good enough repair. It wouldn't take much to make Rapper and Nellie comfortable, and in fact they'd lived in tents for their last stay in the county. It had been raining then, too, as Rhodes recalled, and he thought they might have learned enough from that experience to look for accommodations that were a little bit more resistant to the elements.

The first two houses Rhodes checked were dark and lonely. On the first, the roof had fallen into rooms and there were no windowpanes left. It might have been a comfortable home at one time, but no one would be living there again.

The second house had a roof but no floor. It was an

old wooden structure built up on stone blocks, and something—termites, maybe—had destroyed the flooring.
Rhodes stood by a window and played the flashlight
beam over the place where the floor had been. On the
rough ground there were a couple of trash heaps that
hadn't been made recently. A rat scuttled out of one of
them and ran from under the house into the weedy field
behind it.

The third house he checked had a light in the front
windows. It looked like fluorescent light, though Rhodes
doubted that there was any electricity running to the
house.

Out in back of the house was a ramshackle chicken
house built of corrugated tin. It was plenty big enough
to hold a couple of motorcycles.

Rhodes stopped the car at the fence in front of the
house and gave his light bar a short buzz. There was a
brief whine from the siren, and red and blue and white
light flickered over the dark exterior of the house.

Rhodes stepped out of the car. "Hello, the house," he
called.

There was no answer, but after a minute the door
opened and someone limped out onto the front porch.

"Hello, Rapper," Rhodes said.

Rhodes had no idea where Rapper had gotten his
name. He'd had it long before the hip-hop nation had
given the word its current meaning, and Rhodes was sure
that Rapper couldn't make a rhyme even if he were so
inclined, which he most certainly never would be.

Rapper was short, not more than five-seven in his motorcycle boots, with a beer-barrel belly and graying hair
that he combed straight back from his forehead in a sort
of satanic V. As Rhodes was well aware, Rapper always

avoided telling the truth if he could think of a plausible lie. Or even an implausible one.

"Good evening, Sheriff," Rapper said. "Nice of you to come calling on us. Don't you think so, Nellie?"

Rhodes could see Nellie standing behind Rapper in the doorway. The origin of Nellie's name was as much a mystery to Rhodes as Rapper's. Nellie was thin but fit, with slicked-back hair that Rhodes thought might have had a touch of Nice 'n' Easy in it, or something similar, though he couldn't be sure. No one of Rhodes's acquaintance had seen Nellie buying hair coloring in Wal-Mart.

"We're always glad to see our old friend the sheriff," Rapper said, talking to Rhodes as much as to Nellie. "Why, if it weren't for him, I might still be able to run a fast quarter mile on the track." He held up his hand and showed off the fingers with the missing tips. "Or I might even still have all my fingers."

Nellie grinned but didn't say anything.

"If you'd stay out of Blacklin County, you wouldn't get into so much trouble," Rhodes told them. "It might be a good idea for you to leave now, before I have to arrest you for trespassing."

"Now, that wouldn't be very friendly, Sheriff," Rapper said. "And you'd be making a big mistake. Nellie and I aren't trespassing. Right, Nellie?"

"Not us," Nellie said. "We're as legal as the day is long, just the way we always are."

Rhodes didn't think that either of them had more than a nodding acquaintance with legality. He said, "You mean you're paying rent on this house?"

"Didn't I tell you the sheriff was a smart man, Nellie?" Rapper said. "Didn't I tell you how sharp he was?"

"You sure did," Nellie said. "He's a regular Eckstine."

"That's *Einstein,*" Rapper said. "Eckstine was some old-time singer or something."

"Oh," Nellie said. "Well, I'll bet the sheriff can sing, too. Ain't that right, Sheriff?"

"You know I'm going to check up on that rental business," Rhodes said, ignoring Nellie's remarks.

"Oh, sure," Rapper said. "We know that. We'd expect you to do that. That's part of your job. You know who owns this old house?"

"This is the old Jenkins place," Rhodes said. He wasn't as good at this sort of thing as Hack was, but he did happen to know about this particular house. "The house belonged to Daniel Jenkins first and then to his son Joel. Belongs to Joel's son Thomas now. Thomas lives in Houston."

"Smart," Nellie said. "Just like you told me, Rapper. Eckstine ain't got nothing on him."

"Einstein," Rapper said.

"Whatever."

"Yeah. Anyway, Sheriff, we got a rental agreement all signed and everything. We've leased this place for a month, and we're gonna stay right here that whole time. Maybe do a little sightseeing, take a tour of the courthouse, you know the kind of thing."

"That's pretty funny, Rapper," Rhodes said. "You should have your own TV show."

"I thought you'd like it. Anyway, if that's all you wanted to know from us, you might as well be moving along. Nellie and I, we were thinking about going to bed. It's late, and we need our sleep if we're gonna get up early to start seeing the sights."

"You know a man named Ty Berry?" Rhodes asked.

"Ty Berry? Sounds familiar. Seems like we might've

run across him the last time we were here for a visit. Why? He giving guided tours of the courthouse now?''

"Never mind. We still have some old charges against the two of you, attempted murder of a peace officer, little things like that. I'll be back with a warrant tomorrow.''

"You come right ahead, Sheriff,'' Rapper said. He smiled. "We've talked to a lawyer about our rights and all that, and you can arrest us if you want to. But we'll be right back out here in our little rent-house before a cat can lick its ass. You do whatever you feel like you have to do, though.''

Rhodes knew that Rapper was right. He could arrest them, and maybe even hold them for a while, but they'd be out in a few hours at the most.

"You've got a point,'' he said. "Maybe I'd better just let you stay here where I can keep an eye on you. That way you might not get into so much trouble.''

"You're not thinking of depriving us of any of our rights, are you?'' Rapper asked.

"Not me,'' Rhodes said. "I wouldn't dream of it.'' He started toward his car, then turned around. "You two enjoy your stay here in Blacklin County.''

"We will,'' Rapper said. "You can count on that.''

Rhodes could feel Rapper's eyes on his back all the way to the car.

FOURTEEN

RHODES WENT BACK to the jail and wrote out his reports. Hack was watching David Letterman on the little black and white TV set on his desk.

"I don't much like it that Letterman's stopped giving out that Top Ten list right at eleven o'clock," Hack said. "You never can tell when he's gonna do it now. It might be as late as eleven-twenty or so."

Rhodes didn't much care. He didn't often get to watch Letterman. He took some arrest forms out of his desk drawer and got to work.

"All that'd be easier to do on a computer," Hack said. "You have the form already right there in front of you, and you don't have to do all the pencil work."

Rhodes had so far resisted the lure of the computer, though Hack had taught him enough about one to make him comfortable with word processing. Sooner or later he'd have to learn even more, since he was contemplating buying a computer of his own, if only because the Internet would help him locate parts for the Edsel.

"You could be right," he said. "I'll talk to the commissioners about getting one for me and the deputies."

"If you don't solve Ty Berry's murder, they won't speak to you," Hack said.

"You could be right about that, too. Did Ruth find anything in his pickup?"

"Not that she told me about. And Buddy didn't find out a thing, either. His report should be on your desk with Ruth's."

Rhodes's desk wasn't exactly a model of neatness. He shuffled through the papers that covered it and located the deputies' reports. Hack was right. They hadn't learned a thing, though Ruth wasn't through with the pickup yet.

"What about Dr. White?" Rhodes asked.

"He called about a half hour before you got here. Said he'd see you in the mornin'. You know what time it is?"

Rhodes looked over at Hack's TV set, where Letterman was reading the Top Ten list for the evening.

"I'd guess around eleven-twenty," he said.

"Pretty close to it. You oughta go on home. Maybe clean yourself up a little before Ivy sees you."

Ivy was getting used to having Rhodes come in late, though she didn't seem to like it much. And she particularly didn't like it when he came in late and beaten up.

"I had a run-in with a tombstone," Rhodes said.

"See any ghosts?"

"I'm not sure. I saw something."

"Did it look like a ghost?"

"You mean like Casper?"

"If that's what a ghost looks like, that's what I mean."

"It didn't look like Caspar," Rhodes said. "It didn't look like much of anything. I was too faraway from it, and it was moving fast."

"A ghost would move fast, I guess, not havin' much weight to slow it down. Be all right with you if Lawton tells the inmates that the ghost is hauntin' the cemetery now instead of the jail? Sure would quiet things down around here if they thought that ghost was gone."

"You think they'll fall for that?" Rhodes asked.

"They're in jail, ain't they?" Hack said. "How smart can they be?"

"You might have a point there," Rhodes admitted. "They're no Ecksteins."

"Huh?" Hack said.

"Never mind," Rhodes said. "You had to be there. Go ahead and give it a try."

"Not me," Hack said. "That's Lawton's job. Or maybe you should do it. It might be they'd take it better if it came from the sheriff."

It was after lights-out, so Rhodes said, "I'll do it in the morning."

"Good enough," Hack said.

WHEN RHODES ARRIVED HOME, Yancey charged out of the kitchen, yapping and yipping. No burglar was ever going to get past him.

Rhodes went on into the living room, where Ivy was reading a romance novel: *Wild Texas Wind*.

Yancey trailed along behind, but he quit yapping when he saw Ivy, who held up the cover of the book so Rhodes could get a better look at it. Yancey wasn't interested in the book at all. He turned around and went back to the kitchen.

"I might be wanting to file a lawsuit against that publisher," Rhodes said. "It looks like they've taken a picture of my body and put some other guy's face on it."

"That 'other guy' is Terry Don Coslin," Ivy said. "And I'll bet you could strike a match on those pecs. You've heard of him, I'll bet."

Rhodes had to admit it. Terry Don Coslin was Blacklin County's most famous resident. After graduating from Clearview High School ten years earlier, he'd gone to college in Dallas, where someone from a modeling agency had seen him. The rest was paperback history.

"His hair's longer than I remember," Rhodes said. "That's what threw me off."

"Sure. And guess who the book's by."

Rhodes looked at the cover again.

"Ashley Leigh," he said.

"Guess again."

"I don't need to guess again. It says 'Ashley Leigh' right there on the front of the book."

"Yes, but that's not her real name. So guess again."

"Not Vernell Lindsey," Rhodes said.

"You got it." Ivy smiled. "She's finally made the big time."

Vernell was a friend of Ivy's, and she had been writing romance novels for as long as Rhodes could remember. She must have written twenty or thirty. She went to conferences all over the country to meet other writers and editors. But as far as Rhodes knew, she'd never actually sold anything.

"Are you sure?"

"Of course I'm sure. She brought it by after you dropped me off. She was so proud I thought she'd pop. She's been disappointed so many times, she didn't want to tell anyone she'd sold it until she had the actual book in her hands. And now here it is."

"Well, good for her," Rhodes said. "How is it?"

He was looking at the cover more closely. Terry Don Coslin was holding a woman with hair even longer than his own in a position that looked to Rhodes to be a bit awkward for both of them. But it had the advantage of exposing a considerable length of the woman's legs. And her low-cut dress exposed a considerable portion of the rest of her.

"It's great," Ivy said. "Oh, I know the cover's kind of hot, but the book's nothing like that. Vernell's a real

student of Texas history, and the book's very accurate as
far as I can tell.''

"Didn't Terry Don Coslin change his name, too?"
Rhodes asked.

"Not really. He just dropped the *Coslin* off. He's Terry
Don now.''

"I wonder if I could get me a job holding pretty
women like that for money,'' Rhodes said.

Ivy got out of the chair, dropped the book in it, and
started toward Rhodes.

"I don't think I'll allow that,'' she said.

THE NEXT MORNING came all too early, as mornings had
a way of doing. Rhodes wanted to do at least two things
before noon: visit Richard Rascoe and talk to Dr. White.
He finished his shredded wheat and skim milk while Yancey nipped at his ankles. He took the cereal bowl to the
sink, rinsed it out, and put it in the dishwasher before
going into the bedroom to say good-bye to Ivy, who was
drying her hair. Then he went outside, with Yancey hot
on his heels.

There were plenty of people now who thought of
Texas as an urban state, made up mostly of big cities like
Dallas, Houston, and San Antonio. It was probably true
that most of the population lived in places like that, and
of course even in places like Clearview there were elements of urban life that hadn't been there when Rhodes
was growing up. But small towns still existed, even if
they weren't thriving. Rhodes was never more aware of
that fact than when he went out into his yard early in the
morning.

He could stand there for a long time and not hear a
single sound other than a sparrow in the pecan trees or
the wind in the leaves. No sound of traffic, no voices

shouting in the streets. And then he might hear something after all, a rooster crowing, or maybe the bleating of a goat. Not exactly the kind of thing you'd hear in an urban setting, he thought.

He took a deep breath of air that he liked to think was just as free of pollution as any in the state, and in fact as free of it as air had been a hundred years ago. He knew he was kidding himself, but at least there was no chemical smell such as he'd experienced on his trips to the Gulf Coast or to the Dallas area.

Not that there was anything wrong with places like that if people wanted to live in them. Rhodes just couldn't see their attraction.

He had a short romp with Speedo and Yancey, who seemed to enjoy it even more than the larger dog, though he was ready to go back inside when Rhodes opened the door. Rhodes let him in and got on his way.

HE CALLED DR. WHITE from the jail. White confirmed that the bullet that had killed Ty Berry came from a .22-caliber weapon, probably a revolver fired at close range.

"No powder burns, though," White said. "So it's not like they were face-to-face. And you can have the bullet if you want it, but it won't help you any. It doesn't have any shape left at all."

"What about powder burns on his hand?"

"Not a trace."

Rhodes thanked him and hung up the phone. Lawton reminded him that he was supposed to tell the prisoners about the ghost, so he went into the cellblock and let them know that there wouldn't be anymore haunting in the jail.

"You right sure about that, Sheriff?" Lank Rollins

asked. "I thought I felt a cold chill pass over me last night."

"That was just the weather," Rhodes assured him. "Four people saw that ghost out at the cemetery last night, and I saw something, too."

Rollins wanted to know what it looked like.

"Nothing much," Rhodes said. "It was like a shadow, didn't have much shape at all."

"That's it, all right," Rollins said. "Tell you the truth, I'm glad it's moved out of here. Ghosts belong in the graveyard, not in any jailhouse."

"You're well acquainted with graveyards, are you?" Rhodes said.

"What do you mean?" Rollins asked.

"I was just wondering if you might know something about who's taking things out of the cemeteries around the county. If you did, you might be able to help us out."

"Not me," Rollins said. "I stay away from graveyards. Not my kinda place at all."

"All right," Rhodes said. "But if anything occurs to you, let Lawton know."

"I'll sure do that, Sheriff," Rollins said, with all the sincerity of a used-car salesman.

RHODES WENT BACK to the office and let Hack and Lawton know that he'd done his duty with the prisoners.

"They believe you?" Lawton asked.

"I think so. Hard to tell with that bunch, though."

"That's the truth," Hack said. "They've told so many lies themselves they wouldn't know the truth if it bit 'em in the butt."

Rhodes told Hack and Lawton that he was going to drive down to Thurston and asked if there'd been any calls that morning.

"Just one," Hack said, with a glance at Lawton.

Rhodes knew what that meant. They wanted him to ask what the call had been about rather than just telling him. He might have tested their resolve, but he didn't have time.

He said, "What about?"

"It was about Vernell Lindsey," Hack said.

Rhodes didn't have to hear anymore than that. He knew what the trouble was. But he didn't say so.

"I was just talking to Ivy about her last night," he said. "She finally sold a book. Ivy has a copy of it."

"Seen it," Hack said. "*Wild Texas Wind.* Got Terry Don Coslin on the cover."

Since Hack hardly ever left the jail, Rhodes could never figure out where he got all his news.

"And it's got a woman, too," Lawton said. "Not Miz Lindsey, though."

"And it don't have her goats, either," Hack said.

The goats were the crux of the problem. Vernell Lindsey had three of them, named Shirley, Goodness, and Mercy.

"Which one's loose this time?" Rhodes asked.

"Shirley," Hack said.

"Jumped the fence again?"

"You got it. You can't fence in a goat. Ever'body knows that."

Everybody except Vernell, Rhodes thought. He said, "Tell Ruth to take care of it. I have to go down to Thurston."

"Can she shoot it?" Hack asked.

"I don't think that would be a good idea. Tell her to handle it with kid gloves."

"Kid gloves," Hack said. "You know, Sheriff, I think

marryin' Ivy's been real good for you. You might even develop a sense of humor.''

"I don't get it," Lawton said.

"Let Hack explain it," Rhodes said, and headed for the door.

FIFTEEN

WHEN RHODES REACHED for the doorknob, the door swung open and almost hit him in the face. Faye Knape came inside so fast that she bumped into him.

"I'm sorry, Sheriff," she said, stepping back and not sounding very sorry at all. "I hope you weren't leaving. I have some important information."

"I was leaving," Rhodes said. "But I can stick around if you have something to tell me."

"I don't," Faye said. "But Sharon does."

Sharon Carlisle was standing behind Faye, just outside the doorway.

"All right," Rhodes said. "Come on in."

He walked over to his desk. There was already a chair beside it, and he pulled up another one for Sharon, who was much shorter than Faye and about ten years younger. She had large eyes and a small nose.

"Have a seat," Rhodes told them.

"This won't take long," Faye said. "You were asking about how I could prove Ty Berry was connected to Richard Rascoe. Well, here's how. Tell him, Sharon."

"All right," Sharon began. She had a deep voice that didn't seem to go with her size. "What happened was—"

Faye interrupted. "What happened was that she was going into Richard Rascoe's store on Monday, and she saw Ty Berry there."

"Is that true?" Rhodes asked.

Sharon nodded. "Yes—"

"Of course it's true!" Faye Knape said. "Why would

she make up something like that? She was going into the store and she saw Ty Berry coming out of that back room where Rascoe is hiding the angel. Isn't that right, Sharon?''

"Yes," Sharon said. "You see—"

"There!" Faye Knape said. "Didn't I tell you? It's exactly like I said it was. Ty and Rascoe were working together all the time!"

"I think it would be a good idea to let Ms. Carlisle tell the story herself," Rhodes said.

Faye sat up and crossed her arms. "Well, I never."

Rhodes ignored her. "Go ahead, Ms. Carlisle."

She told the story pretty much the way Faye Knape had. She had been looking for "something cute for Easter," and she'd heard about Rascoe's store. So she decided to pay it a visit.

"Tell him about seeing Ty Berry," Faye Knape said. "Tell him about how Ty was in that back room."

Sharon looked at Rhodes and rolled her eyes. Rhodes tried not to smile.

"It's true," Sharon said. "I was looking at this little tea set that had Easter bunnies on the teapot and cups, and I saw Ty Berry coming out of that back room."

"Did he seem upset?" Rhodes asked.

"Of course he was upset!" Faye said. "Wouldn't you be upset if someone had caught you in the act?"

Rhodes looked at Sharon.

"Well, he didn't look upset to me," she said. "He just looked the way he always did, a little worried, maybe, but not upset."

Faye took a deep breath, but Rhodes headed her off.

"Did he say anything to you?" he asked Sharon.

"No. Well, he said, 'Good morning,' or something like that, but we didn't have a conversation or anything."

"And did he talk to Mr. Rascoe?"

"I don't know. I didn't see Mr. Rascoe until later."

"And do you know why?" Faye Knape asked.

Rhodes didn't know, but he was sure that Faye was going to tell him. And she didn't disappoint.

"She didn't see him," Faye said, "because he was in the back room, where he and Ty had been making their deal. He was probably gloating over getting that angel."

"You don't know that," Rhodes said.

"Oh, but I do."

"How?"

Faye Knape looked at Rhodes as if he might be somehow mentally deficient.

"Because it has to be that way," she said, as if stating something that would be obvious even to a child. "Otherwise, why would Ty Berry have been there? He and Rascoe were back in that room making one of their shady deals, like they've been doing all along. They're in cahoots! Ty was stealing things, and Rascoe was buying them."

Rhodes nodded just as if she were making sense. He'd learned long ago that a nod didn't really commit him to anything. If people wanted to think he was agreeing with them, that was their business.

"I'll be going down to Thurston today," he said. "I'll have a little talk with Rascoe and see what he knows."

"He knows plenty," Faye said. "You mark my words. Come on, Sharon."

They got up and left. Rhodes watched them go, slightly in awe of Faye Knape. In spite of all his experiences with people over the years, he could still be amazed at the different ways they could convince themselves that they were the only ones in the parade who were marching in step.

"Now that she's solved your case for you," Hack said, "what're you gonna do for the rest of the day?"

"Maybe I should just go home and take a nap," Rhodes said.

THURSTON HAD BEEN well on the way to becoming like Milsby before someone came up with the idea of lining its main street with antique stores. Hob Barrett's grocery store sat between two of the refurbished buildings, unchanged. It still had the faded Rainbo Bread signs stenciled on its screen doors, and it still had the same old Coca-Cola cooler, from which Rhodes took a Dr Pepper that was wet and frigid in his hand. He walked to the counter and paid Hob fifty cents.

"How's business?" Rhodes asked.

"It's been better," Hob said, putting the two quarters in an old cash register that would have looked right at home in one of the antique stores. "What brings you down here?"

"Looking at antiques," Rhodes said.

He took a sip of the Dr Pepper, which was very cold. Rhodes could feel it all the way down his throat.

"I hope you ain't doin' it on county time," Hob said.

Hob was short and stout, a little like an anvil on legs, and he didn't much like Rhodes, even though Rhodes had solved the murder of his wife not so very long ago.

"I was just making conversation," Rhodes said. "Antiques are connected with a case I'm working on."

"Humpf," Barrett said, clearly not believing a word of it.

"Do you know your neighbor, Mr. Rascoe?" Rhodes asked.

"Not much. He's a city fella, doesn't live here and

doesn't buy anything from me. Prob'ly goes to one of those big HEB stores somewhere."

Rhodes figured that, in Hob's book, buying from a chain store like HEB would be a sizable crime. Rhodes could remember the days in Clearview when there had been little mom-and-pop groceries every two or three blocks. Now there wasn't a single one. They'd all been replaced by a chain of convenience stores with headquarters in some city like Dallas or Houston. And of course there was an HEB supermarket.

Rhodes drank some more of the Dr Pepper, then said, "You ever go in Rascoe's store?"

"Hell, no. Why would I want to do that? He won't come in here, and he doesn't have a damn thing I want over there. What about you? Need anything besides that Dr Pepper?"

Rhodes was about to say that he didn't, but he changed his mind.

"How about a can of Vienna sausage and some crackers?" he said.

"I'll get 'em," Hob said.

He went to the shelves and got a small can of sausages and a box of crackers.

"More crackers here than you'll need," he said, setting them on the counter.

"I don't mind," Rhodes said, paying him.

While Hob put the groceries in a sack, Rhodes stuck the Dr Pepper bottle in a wooden case sitting by the Coke box. Then he got his sack and left.

RICHARD RASCOE'S STORE had once been Thurston's drugstore, though you couldn't tell it now, not unless you recognized the tiled floor. There was no sign of the soda fountain or the red vinyl-covered round stools that spun around on their chrome poles.

That was too bad, Rhodes thought. The fountain would have been a nice touch for an antique store.

On the other hand, Rascoe had plenty of antiques without it. Or maybe they weren't antiques, not by any strict definition of the term. Rhodes wondered what the right word would be. *Collectibles,* maybe.

There was one display case that held baseball cards and Dixie cup tops. There was one shelf full of soft drink bottles and several that held all kinds of glassware. There were churns and crocks. Several boxes of different kinds of barbed wire. Old costume jewelry. On an end table sat a tea set like the one described by Sharon Carlisle, decorated with colorful Easter bunnies. Or maybe they were just plain bunnies. Rhodes didn't know the difference. In one corner there was a traffic light on a short pole, and sitting nearby was a barber chair. There was a shelf of dusty old books that didn't look as if they'd been touched in years. There were quilts on a quilt rack, and old rocking chairs, and even a rack of old clothes. The whole place had a musty, dusty smell that Rhodes liked.

He looked at the Dixie cup tops for a minute or so. He especially liked the one with the picture of Roy Rogers on it.

"See anything you need?" someone said behind him.

Rhodes turned around. "You must be Mr. Rascoe," he said.

Rascoe stuck out a hand. "That's me. And you are?"

"Sheriff Dan Rhodes."

Rhodes shook Rascoe's hand. The antique dealer had a firm grip that went with his lean, tanned features. He looked like a man who either spent some time out-of-doors or in a tanning booth. Forced to make a choice,

Rhodes would have gone with the tanning booth. Aside from the tan, Rascoe didn't seem to be the outdoors type.

"What brings you to my little store, Sheriff?" Rascoe asked, releasing Rhodes's hand.

"Ty Berry," Rhodes said, watching Rascoe closely.

"Ah, the good Mr. Berry. Has he told you about something here you'd like to see?"

"He mentioned an angel."

"I have a couple of those," Rascoe said. "There's one right over there."

He pointed to an angelic figure made of pieces of stained glass. The figure was probably Gabriel, Rhodes thought, since it was blowing a horn.

"That's not the one," he said. "The one I'm talking about is the kind you find in cemeteries."

"Oh, that one," Rascoe said. "It's in the back room, but you're welcome to look at it if you'd like."

Rhodes said he'd like, and Rascoe led the way to a room in the back of the store. Just as Faye Knape had said, there was a sign on the door saying, EMPLOYEES ONLY.

Rascoe pushed open the door and said, "Here it is, right over there."

He pointed to a stone angel that sat on top of a cedar chest that was mostly covered by a blue blanket.

"It just came in the other day," Rascoe said, "and it's already sold. That's why it's back here instead of out there with the rest of the stock. But if you want it, I can get you another one just like it."

"Where?" Rhodes asked.

"I'd have to look for the catalog," Rascoe said. "It's somewhere down around Houston, I think. I can get it within a couple of days."

Rhodes looked the angel over and touched its head.

"So this is brand new," he said.

"Well, almost. I've had it for a week or so."

"And Ty Berry saw it here."

"That's right. He thought it was a nice example of what people are doing these days, and I agree that the craftsmanship is excellent."

"I'd like to see that catalog," Rhodes said, not exactly sure that *craftsmanship* was the right word to use, since the angel seemed to be a mass-production item.

"Catalog?" Rascoe said. "Sure thing. It might take me a minute to find it. Just have a look around the store, and I'll be right with you."

Rhodes went back into the main part of the store and admired the Dixie cup tops for a few minutes while Rascoe rummaged around in a rolltop desk in the back. Before long, Rascoe came up to Rhodes with a catalog in his hand.

"Here it is," Rascoe said. "Benson's Concrete Works. They have birdbaths, statues, porch steps, you name it. If it's made out of concrete, they have it."

Rhodes flipped through the catalog and found the page with the angels on it.

"Mind if I keep this?" he said.

Rascoe looked puzzled. "I suppose not. I can get another one. Does this have something to do with a crime?"

Rhodes stuck the catalog in a back pocket.

"You never can tell," he said.

SIXTEEN

THERE WAS STILL plenty of time before noon, and Rhodes had accomplished both of the things he'd set out to do. He wasn't sure he was any wiser than before, but he was in motion if not making progress. Since he had time, he thought it might be a good idea to stop by the library and do a little research.

The library's official name was the Clarence P. Mullin Memorial Library, though no one called it that. Everyone in Clearview referred to it simply as "the library," since, after all, it was the only one in town. For that matter, it was the only one in the county.

Clarence P. Mullin had been a farmer before oil was struck on his land during the early part of the century. The story was told that after coming into more money than he'd ever dreamed of, Mullin had told his friends that he wanted to do something for the town of Clearview, where he'd grown up and gone to school. The friends had asked what he thought the town needed more than anything, and he'd said that it needed a library. "So why don't you build one?" they asked, and he had. Not only that, but he'd endowed it, which Rhodes thought was a good thing, the way the county commissioners were always worrying over their budget. They couldn't touch the library money, so there was always something in the budget for books, upkeep of the building, and even improvements.

Rhodes parked the county car and went inside. Milli-cent Conway was working at the desk, just as she had been ever since Rhodes could remember. She had faded blue eyes, faded red hair, and hands that were beginning to tremble a little because of her age. But her mind was just as sharp as it had always been.

"Good morning, Sheriff," she said as Rhodes walked up to the desk. "What can we do for you today? Do you need a good book to read?"

Rhodes was tempted to ask if she had a copy of *Wild Texas Wind,* but he didn't. He said, "I need to find out something about history."

"Well, we certainly have plenty of history books. We have books on world history, United States history, Texas history, and even the history of Blacklin County. Which one would you be interested in?"

"The one that would tell me what happened in A.D. 11," Rhodes said.

"You probably don't know the Library of Congress classification system, do you?" she said.

"You're right," Rhodes said. "I don't."

"Well, I'll show you, then."

She took him to the shelves where the world history books were lined up.

"If I were you, I'd begin with Rome," she said, and left him on his own.

He pulled several books off the shelves and took them over to a table to look through them. He spent thirty minutes or so flipping the pages, but he didn't find anything helpful. It appeared that nothing of importance to the world had happened in A.D. 11, or if it had, Rhodes couldn't locate it.

He learned that Ovid had been banished by the Roman emperor Augustus at around that time, though not during that year, and that the Hsin Dynasty had been in power in China. Rhodes didn't see how any of that was going to help him.

There was a sign that asked browsers not to reshelve books, so Rhodes left them on the table and went to the desk to thank Miss Conway for her help.

"You didn't find anything, did you?" she said.

"No. It must have been a pretty dull year."

"That's what I thought. Why were you looking?"

"I thought it might be a clue," Rhodes said.

"Well, I hope you figure it out."

"Me, too," Rhodes said.

AFTER LEAVING THE LIBRARY, Rhodes drove to the City Park and sat on a bench under a shade tree to have lunch. He stuck a finger in the ring-tab and pulled back the top of the can of sausages, which appeared to be packed in pure fat. He got one out of the can and ate it and a couple of crackers with genuine satisfaction. It didn't take him long to finish the whole can, which he disposed of in a nearby trash container. He dusted off his hands and leaned back on the bench.

There was no one in the park to disturb him, though there was a squirrel running around looking for something or other in the grass. It was a warm day, and Rhodes let his mind wander, trying to think of all the things he knew about Ty Berry and who might have a motive to kill him.

For some reason, Rhodes kept circling back to Rapper and Nellie. Whenever they turned up in the county, there was trouble, and they were always connected to it. It might be that they had something to do with things, but for the life of him, Rhodes couldn't figure out what they were up to. He was going to have to do a little nosing around, see if he could find out what they were doing.

On both of their previous visits, there'd been a drug connection, first marijuana and then steroids. He wondered if they'd discovered a new kind of illegal substance to peddle. It sounded just like them. They seemed to think that they could get away with just about anything in Blacklin County, and so far they'd been proved right, not counting a few broken ribs, a few missing fingers, and a slight limp. Sooner or later, though, Rhodes knew he'd get them and send them where they belonged, which was to one of the stricter units of the Texas Department of Criminal Justice. One of the maximum-security prisons down around Houston would be a good place, he thought. Rapper and Nellie would do fine there.

And then there was Faye Knape.

He realized that he'd made a big mistake, thanks to his easygoing nature. It wasn't the first time it had happened, and it certainly wouldn't be the last.

Instead of taking charge of the conversation, he'd let Mrs. Knape lead it where she wanted it to go. When she'd asked if he'd come to talk to her about Ty Berry, he should have taken the initiative and begun questioning her about her whereabouts the previous evening. But he'd let her take things in an entirely different direction. She'd neatly deflected any suspicion from herself and onto Richard Rascoe and even onto Berry. Besides that, she had Rhodes following up on her leads and ignoring her completely.

Well, he couldn't let her get away with that. He got up, stretched, and walked over to the county car. It was time to go to the jail.

RUTH GRADY SAID there hadn't been any difficulty with the goats.

"Shirley hadn't gone far," she said. "And she wasn't hard to catch. I roped her."

Hack was impressed. He'd been opposed to Ruth's hiring when Rhodes brought her into the department, but she'd quickly won him over.

"You carry a rope with you?" he said. "How long you been doin' that?"

"Ever since Ms. Lindsey's goats started jumping that low fence of hers," Ruth said.

"Who taught you how to rope?"

"I learned it from my daddy when I was a little girl. He used to watch me practice out in the back yard."

"Can you do any tricks?"

"I can twirl a loop, but that's about it. I'm no Will Rogers."

"About the goat," Rhodes said.

Ruth smiled. She was as prone to being distracted by Hack and Lawton as Rhodes was.

"I talked to Ms. Lindsey about putting up a higher fence," she said. "Again. I don't think I made much of an impression this time, either. She wasn't really listening. All she could talk about was her book."

"Did she show you a copy?" Hack asked.

"Better than that. She gave me one."

"What'd you think of the cover?"

"Not bad. Hard to believe that somebody as good-looking as Terry Don actually went to school right here in Clearview."

Hack was offended. "What do you mean by that? I went to school here."

"I hadn't thought of that," Ruth said. "It's even harder to believe that you and he both could have gone to school here. Wow. Two hunks from the same small town."

Hack grinned and nodded just as if he believed her.

"The goats," Rhodes said.

"Oh. Right. Goodness and Mercy were still inside the fence, and Shirley's there now, too. Doesn't mean they'll stay there, though. She really ought to get a higher fence."

"Or get rid of them goats," Hack said. "You'd think we'd have some kind of ordinance around here against havin' animals in the yard."

"They're not in the yard, exactly," Ruth said. "It's more like a field."

"She lives inside the city limits," Hack said, "so it's a yard."

"I guess you're right."

"There's no ordinance, though," Rhodes said, "So we don't have to worry about it. We're not going to be able to arrest her, no matter what Hack thinks. What about Ty Berry's pickup? Did you find anything?"

"No," Ruth said. "His fingerprints, of course." She looked at Rhodes. "And yours."

"Sorry," Rhodes said.

"There were those two notes, too," Ruth said. "But you saw those."

"What did you make of them?"

"Not much. You?"

Rhodes told her about Ovid and the Hsin Dynasty.

"That's a big help," Hack said. "I bet he was killed by somebody named Augustus, and that's some kind of dying message. You know anybody named that?"

Rhodes said that he didn't.

"What about Hsin? Any Hsins in Clearview?"

Rhodes said he didn't think so.

"Me neither," Hack said. "You want to try the phone book?"

"Only as a last resort."

"What're you gonna do, then?"

"Ask Faye Knape a few more questions," Rhodes said.

"She won't like it. You got anything else in mind?"

"Searching Ty's house," Rhodes said. "You call over there and see if his cousin's come in from Austin. If she has, tell her I'm coming over."

"What if she's not there?"

"Then I'm going over anyway," Rhodes said.

SEVENTEEN

NOT ONLY DID Faye Knape not like being questioned, she was highly offended. Not to mention indignant, insulted, red-faced, and irate.

"Well, I never!" she said when Rhodes asked her about her whereabouts the night Berry had died. "I can't believe you have the nerve to ask me such a question!"

They were sitting in the same room where they'd been on the previous evening, but so far Rhodes hadn't sneezed. His nose was itching, however, and he knew it wouldn't be long.

"I'm sorry that I have to," he said. "But I have to follow every lead in something like this."

"Lead?" Faye was even more indignant. "What lead?"

"Ty Berry didn't have many enemies. In fact, you're about the only one I can think of. So naturally I'd like to establish that you have an alibi. That way I can eliminate you as a suspect."

Faye practically leapt off the couch. Rhodes took the opportunity to sneeze. He grabbed a tissue and used it.

"Alibi!" Faye Knape said. "Suspect! You must be crazy!"

"I wouldn't be surprised," Rhodes said.

"Don't joke with me! How dare you accuse me of killing anyone!"

"I wasn't accusing you. I was just saying that you're a logical suspect."

"Well, that's where you're wrong. I argued with Ty

Berry about a lot of things; and I have to admit that I think he was stealing from the cemeteries, but I never killed him. He did that himself.''

"I don't think so," Rhodes said.

"You could be wrong."

"Maybe." Rhodes sneezed again. "But it doesn't look that way. He hadn't fired a pistol."

"He was in cahoots with that Rascoe."

"I'm not so sure about that, either," Rhodes said. "I talked to Richard Rascoe about that angel you saw. He says it's new. He ordered it from this catalog."

Rhodes pulled the catalog from his back pocket and showed her the angel. Faye took the catalog from him and studied the picture of the angel carefully.

"It looks like the one I saw," she admitted. "But I'm sure it's not. Ty Berry stole the one I saw and sold it to Rascoe. I caught them in the act."

"I think you're mistaken," Rhodes said.

Faye took a deep breath. She sat back down and put the catalog on the end table with the Bible, the cut-glass vase with its dried flowers, and the tissues.

"All right," she said. "If you think I'm mistaken, maybe I am. And if you say Ty didn't kill himself, then I'll believe you."

Rhodes thought that was gracious of her, though she didn't sound gracious. She also didn't sound convinced.

"So it was probably Vernell Lindsey who killed Ty," she went on. "Wouldn't you agree?"

"What?"

"Vernell Lindsey. You're the sheriff. You should know about these things."

"What things?"

"Motives for murder. Don't you ever watch the reruns of *Murder, She Wrote?*"

Rhodes admitted that he didn't, and sneezed.

"Well, you should. You could learn a lot about crime-solving from Jessica Fletcher."

Rhodes thought he could also learn a lot from just about anyone. Right now he didn't feel very skilled. He said, "You could be right."

"Of course I'm right. Anyway, one of the main reasons people kill is for love. So there you are."

"Where?" Rhodes asked.

"Vernell and Ty Berry had been keeping company for the last month or two, but they had some kind of big argument and broke up. That's why she killed him."

"Oh," Rhodes said.

And then he realized that he'd let Mrs. Knape do it again. She had never answered his question about where she'd been the night Berry was killed. Instead, she'd led him off on a completely different trail.

So he asked again. "What about your alibi? Where were you when Berry died?"

"Well, I never. You can't mean you want to know that, not after what I just told you."

"I'm afraid I have to know."

"That's fine, then. I have a perfectly good alibi. I was right here at home, which is where I always am, most evenings. Sometimes I go play Chickenfoot with some friends, but I haven't done that lately."

"Chickenfoot?"

"It's a game. Like dominoes, but different."

"I see," Rhodes said, though he didn't. "Was there anyone here with you?"

"Of course."

"Who?"

"The boys."

"The boys?"

"The cats," she said patiently, as if Rhodes were having trouble understanding. Which he was. "The boys are always here with me."

"I don't think I can question them, though," Rhodes said. "And I don't think a judge would accept their statements as an alibi."

"That doesn't matter," she said without irony. "I was here. I didn't kill anyone. I give you my word."

"I appreciate that," Rhodes said, and sneezed. "Do you own a gun?"

"No. I used to own several. They all belonged to my late husband, but I sold them."

"Was one of them a .22 pistol?"

"I don't know. I don't know anything about guns."

Rhodes wasn't sure whether he believed her or not, but for the moment he was going to give her the benefit of the doubt. He had to leave. Either that or start sneezing every other breath.

He thanked her for her time and got out of there.

RHODES DROVE AWAY from Faye Knape's house with one hand on the steering wheel. He was rubbing his eyes with the other hand, which wasn't good for his eyes and which made driving more dangerous than it should be. But he couldn't help it. His eyes were giving him fits.

His interview with Mrs. Knape hadn't been very satisfactory, and it hadn't done much to eliminate her as a suspect. He also knew that the guns her husband had bought wouldn't be registered. Mr. Knape had died years ago, before the new laws had taken effect.

The information about Vernell Lindsey had been in-

teresting, however, and Rhodes radioed Hack that he was
going to pay her a visit.

"About them goats?" Hack asked.

"Not exactly."

"What about Ty Berry's house? You still plannin' to
go by there?"

"Any reason why I shouldn't?"

"Nope. I called the cousin. She's there, and she knows
you're comin' by. It's all quiet around here. No ghosts
or anything like that. You take your time."

Rhodes said that he would.

VERNELL LINDSEY, or Ashley Leigh, lived near the edge
of town in a rambling ranch-style house that had been
built sometime during the 1950s. It was on a half acre of
land, and it had a three-foot chain-link fence around most
of the property in back of the house. It was a good fence.
It just wasn't high enough to contain Shirley, Goodness,
and Mercy.

The fence was in better repair than the house itself,
which could have used some paint. In some places the
fascia boards had rotted and needed replacing. The gut-
ters were rusty and full of leaves from the pecan and
cottonless cottonwood trees that grew in the front yard.
There were more weeds in the yard than grass, though
that wasn't true of the back, where the goats had pretty
much cleared the land. Where the doorbell should have
been, there was a hole with a couple of wires jutting out.

Rhodes wasn't tempted to join the wires and see what
happened. He knocked on the door facing instead.

Vernell Lindsey came to the door looking nothing like
Rhodes would have pictured Ashley Leigh. She had on
faded jeans and a black sweatshirt that had a picture of
Bart Simpson on the front. Her hair, which was as black

as Faye Knape's, was caught back by a huge plastic clip. She wasn't wearing makeup, but then she didn't really need it. She had startlingly blue eyes that went well with the black hair. She wasn't wearing shoes, and her toenails were painted pink.

"It's not the goats again, is it?" she said. "I don't have time to deal with the goats right now. I'm in the middle of a chapter."

"It's not the goats," Rhodes said. "It's Ty Berry."

Vernell's face fell. "What about him?"

"About who killed him."

"It wasn't me."

"That's what we have to talk about."

"Oh, all right. Come on in. I've already lost my train of thought."

She turned around and padded down a dim hallway. Rhodes followed her inside and closed the door.

EIGHTEEN

VERNELL WASN'T MUCH of a housekeeper. Rhodes supposed she spent most of her time writing. The den was littered with newspapers, books, and pieces of computer paper. Some pages of the computer paper had printing on them. Others had handwritten paragraphs. Some were crumpled; others weren't.

"Excuse the mess," Vernell said.

She sat down on the couch, which looked as if it had been there since the house was built, and picked up a package of Winston Lights from the low coffee table in front of it. She didn't ask if Rhodes minded her smoking. She lit her cigarette with a butane lighter, leaned back, and exhaled a stream of white smoke.

"Have a seat, Sheriff. How's Ivy?"

Rhodes shoved aside a newspaper and sat in a platform rocker. He knew the smoke wasn't going to do his eyes any good.

"Ivy's fine. She was reading your book last night. Congratulations."

"Thanks. It's been a long time coming. But I'm on my way now. My agent thinks she can sell some of the ones I've already written, and I'm halfway through a sequel to *Wild Texas Wind*. I don't need somebody like Ty Berry messing things up for me."

"Ty's not able to mess things up for anybody."

Vernell puffed at her cigarette. "You know what I mean. He's dead, and we were friends. So that could be trouble."

For a romance writer, she wasn't very romantic in Rhodes's opinion. A little coldhearted, in fact. She didn't seem to care at all about Ty. She was just worried about herself.

"I know what you're thinking," she said, exhaling smoke in his direction. "You're thinking I should be crying my eyes out over Ty. Well, I'm not. He treated me like dirt, but that doesn't matter now. I've got something better than him. I have a writing career."

"And he's dead," Rhodes reminded her.

"Sure. But that's not my problem. Unless that's why you're here."

Rhodes asked what she meant.

"Unless you're here to make it my problem," she said.

"I might be. But maybe you have an alibi for the night Ty was killed, and I can just go away and leave you alone. Were you with anyone that night?"

"I sure was."

"Good. Who?"

"Zeke Haverford and the beautiful, untamed daughter of Potifair Jones."

"They don't live around here, do they?" Rhodes said.

"They're characters in my new book. I've been working on it for the last month, and I'm here every night doing revisions of what I wrote during the day. When I'm not writing, I'm researching. I don't have time to go out and kill people in cemeteries."

She stubbed out her cigarette in an ashtray shaped like the state of Texas. Smoke writhed upward and Rhodes closed his eyes for a second.

"You and Ty went together for a good while, didn't you?" he asked.

"Define 'a good while.'"

"Months."

"It was probably months. But it doesn't really matter. We just didn't get along. We had a mutual interest in history, but there wasn't anything else between us. No spark. You know what I'm talking about?"

"Sort of," Rhodes said. "Did Ty feel the same way?"

"Yes. We broke up by mutual agreement. We both liked history, as I said, but we didn't like the same books, we didn't like the same movies, we didn't have the same political views, and when it came right down to it, we didn't like each other very much. So we decided to stop seeing each other. Why waste the time?"

"Did he ever mention anyone who might want to kill him?"

"Of course not. Who'd want to do that? We didn't get along all that well, but he was a nice enough guy. You should be able to figure out who killed him. It was whoever's been stealing things from the cemeteries."

"That's what I thought," Rhodes said. "But people keep giving me other ideas."

"And I'll bet I can tell you who gave you the idea it might have been me," Vernell said. "But I won't. I know you wouldn't tell me even if I guessed right."

That was true. Rhodes wasn't in the habit of telling people anymore than they needed to know about his investigations.

"And since I know you can keep a secret," Vernell continued, "I have a little tip for you if you want to look into things besides the cemetery thefts."

"What's that?" Rhodes asked.

Vernell got out another cigarette, lit it, and exhaled more smoke. Rhodes felt his eyes turning redder.

"You should find out who owns those buildings downtown," Vernell said. "The ones that fell down."

Rhodes thought about sitting on his hands. If he didn't,

he was going to start doing some serious eye-rubbing. He resisted both impulses and said, "Why should those buildings interest me?"

"Because they interested Ty. You know why they collapsed, don't you?"

That was an easy one. "Neglect," Rhodes said. "A whole lot of it."

"That's right. No roof repairs for years and years, and that let the rain get in and rot the wood and wash out the grouting and God only knows what else. No upkeep at all. With a little care, they might still be standing there. They could be remodeled into something useful. But there wasn't any care, so they're gone."

"Not exactly," Rhodes said.

"Oh, I didn't mean they're totally gone. But they're not really buildings anymore. All that's there is a pile of rubble."

Rhodes wasn't sure just what the point of the discussion was, so he asked.

"You know how Ty was," Vernell said. "He worried about everything that had any kind of tie to the past, even if it wasn't much of a past to begin with."

Rhodes agreed that Ty was like that.

"Yes. Everyone knew that. He saw what towns like Thurston were doing with their old buildings, and he thought Clearview could do something similar. He thought some kind of renovation might save the downtown area, but it turned out that whoever owned the property here had let things go for too long. It was too late to do anything to save the buildings. The repairs would have been too expensive."

Rhodes admitted the truth of all that she had said, but he still didn't see what any of it could have had to do with Ty Berry's murder.

"That last time I saw him," Vernell said, "he was looking into the possibility of a lawsuit against the owners of the buildings."

"What was he going to sue them for?"

"Do I look like a lawyer?"

Rhodes wasn't sure what a lawyer was supposed to look like. Or a writer, for that matter. So he didn't bother to answer her question. She wasn't expecting one anyway.

And she didn't wait for one. "Reckless endangerment, maybe? The buildings could have fallen on someone. He must've had something in mind."

"So you think the owners killed him?"

"I don't know," Vernell said, puffing on her cigarette. "The last time I talked to him about it, he hadn't been able to find out who the owners were."

That was interesting, Rhodes thought. It should have been easy to find out something like that. Maybe in a city, where some Mafia slumlord was hiding behind dozens of corporate aliases, it would be hard to find out who owned a property. But in Blacklin County, it shouldn't have taken more than a few minutes at the courthouse.

Rhodes stood up and said, "I appreciate your help. I might have to talk to you again before this is over."

Vernell mashed out her cigarette and looked up at him. "Well, try not to interrupt me when I'm writing."

"All right. I hope things work out for Zeke and the beautiful, untamed what's-her-name."

"Maddie."

"Nice name," Rhodes said.

"She's a nice girl," Vernell said. She smiled. "Most of the time."

NINETEEN

RHODES DROVE FROM Vernell's house to the late Ty Berry's place, an old brick home with a neatly trimmed and edged yard that Rhodes envied, considering the usual ragged state of his own lawn.

Berry's cousin answered the door. She was about fifty, short, with blondish hair. She didn't seem overly concerned that Berry was dead. Her name was Cathy Miller.

"He was my cousin on my father's side, and we never saw each other much," she told Rhodes after taking him into a living room that made Vernell Lindsey's look positively slovenly by comparison. Obviously Ty Berry was a man who liked to keep things clean and in perfect order. His pickup had been nearly spotless.

"You knew him, though," Rhodes said.

"Oh, sure. We visited here some when I was a kid. Ty was a little younger than I was, and he was a little priss even then. It's okay to call him a priss, isn't it?"

"I don't mind. But I'm not sure what you mean by it."

"Oh, just that Ty was always afraid to get dirty. Wouldn't even go barefoot in the summertime, didn't want to walk on the ground without his shoes on. Look at this house. Did you ever see anything like it?"

Rhodes looked around. He had known people who were even more obsessed with neatness than Ty had been, but that wasn't what Ty's cousin wanted to hear. So Rhodes said, "I guess not."

"Of course you haven't. Why would anyone want to

kill a man like Ty? All he wanted was to have things in their places and to preserve what he could of the past.''

"I don't know why anyone would kill him," Rhodes said. "That's what I'm trying to find out."

"Well, I'm afraid I can't help you. Ty and I talked about once a year, if that often, and we saw each other even less. I have no idea what might have been going on in his life."

"Is it all right with you if I look around the house?" Rhodes asked.

"Be my guest. But you won't find anything. This place is cleaner than a hound's tooth and twice as slick."

Rhodes thanked her and had a look around anyway. He didn't find anything of interest, however. Berry seemed to have been one of those people who, in spite of his interest in history, didn't hang on to things. There were no collections, unless you counted the five framed pictures of county courthouses. There were only a few clothes hanging in the closets and folded carefully in the chest of drawers. There were some nonfiction books on Texas topics, famous ones like Dobie's *Coronado's Children* and *The Longhorns,* Graves's *Goodbye to a River,* and Lea's *The Brave Bulls,* but they hardly appeared to have been read.

Rhodes flipped through several of them to see if they were valuable first editions. They weren't. The margins occasionally had penciled notes in Berry's hand, but Rhodes couldn't make anything of them. One typical note in *The Brave Bulls* said, "L is R about this."

Rhodes thought a meticulous man like Berry might have kept a diary, but there was no sign of one. There was nothing written down anywhere that would help Rhodes: nothing about cemeteries, about the buildings downtown, about Faye Knape, or about Vernell Lindsey.

He looked at Berry's computer, which was located in a small bedroom that Berry had fixed up as an office. Rhodes didn't know much about computers, but he'd learned enough from Hack to know how to turn it on and search through the word processing program for information relating to cemeteries. He found a good bit, but nothing that was of any use. There were also a number of files relating to the Sons and Daughters of Texas, but none of them was any help. And there was nothing at all about the buildings, Faye, or Vernell. Rhodes thought he might have Ruth come out and check the computer later if he didn't turn up anything in the normal course of the investigation, but for now he'd assume that what he'd found on it was all there was.

Rhodes left the office and thanked Ms. Miller for letting him look through the house.

"You're not going to find out who killed him, are you?" she said.

"Oh, I'll find out," Rhodes said. "I usually do."

She looked at him as if she didn't believe it in the least, but she didn't say anything. So Rhodes went on out to his car.

RHODES SPENT the rest of the afternoon talking to some of the Sons and Daughters of Texas that he hadn't talked to previously. Not a one of them could think of any reason for Ty Berry's death or name a single enemy that he might have had. And like the others Rhodes had interviewed, all of them mentioned that the chief suspects had to be whoever was looting the cemeteries. They were no help at all, so Rhodes went back to the jail to see if anything had happened in his absence.

"Not much," Hack told him. "Unless you count a little wreck or two."

"Anyone hurt?"

"Nope, so I wouldn't count 'em, myself."

"Who handled them?"

"Ruth took care of things."

Rhodes said he wouldn't count them, then. Ruth wouldn't have left any loose ends.

"There's something I want her to check on for me," Rhodes said. "Have her go by the courthouse tomorrow and see who owned those old buildings downtown. The ones that are on the sidewalk now."

"I'll tell her. What's that all about?"

"Ty Berry was looking into it. It might have something to do with what happened to him."

Lawton was lurking around in the background, occasionally pushing his broom. He was clearly listening to the conversation, and Rhodes knew something was going on. He also knew he'd have to wait until Hack and Lawton were ready to tell him what it was. Sooner or later, they would. Rhodes went to his desk and looked around on it for the forms he needed to fill out.

"Ain't you gonna tell him about the ghost?" Lawton asked.

"Not again," Rhodes said.

"Depends on what you mean by *again*," Hack said.

"I mean in the jail."

"Well, it wasn't here," Hack said. "But it's not a different ghost. It's the same one."

"Someone saw it again?"

Lawton shook his head. "Nope."

Rhodes counted to ten under his breath. "What, then?"

"The word's out all over town," Lawton said.

"Yep," Hack said. "Surprised you ain't heard about it."

"I haven't, though," Rhodes said. "And I'm beginning to wonder if I ever will."

Lawton gave Hack a significant look. "Touchy, ain't he? Wonder if ever'thing's all right at home."

Hack sighed and looked at Rhodes. "I hope so. I like Ivy a lot. I'd hate to see anything bust you two up."

"The ghost," Rhodes said. "Tell me about the ghost."

"Oh, yeah. Well, it's the same ghost. It's just that the word on the street is that Ty Berry's come back to haunt the graveyard. Folks're sayin' he'll walk the night until his killer's been brought to justice. They say he told you that last night in the graveyard."

"Told me? When would he do that?"

"When you went out there to talk to him after those kids spotted him. Seems you two had quite a conversation."

"Good grief," Rhodes said.

"Yep," Lawton said. "That's kinda what I thought. But you know how people are, 'specially when something supernatural shows up in the cemetery. Ty's ghost is the talk of the town."

"That's just great," Rhodes said. "I don't suppose you have any other good news you forgot to mention to me."

"Don't think so," Hack said. "Not unless you mean the dope."

Rhodes sat up straighter in his chair. "Dope? What dope? As in drugs?"

"You said you weren't gonna count them wrecks," Hack said. "Remember?"

Someday, Rhodes thought, he was probably going to strangle Hack. But when he did, what would the county do for a dispatcher? They were never going to find someone like Hack, someone who didn't have much of a life outside the jail, who was willing to work for a small wage, and who even slept in the jail most nights to be sure he was there when the calls came in. So Rhodes would control himself.

"Maybe I made a mistake," he said.

"Could be," Lawton said.

"Sure could," Hack said to Rhodes. "You never know what's gonna be in some car that's been in a wreck. I remember one time you found a pistol lyin' in the front seat of a car that'd had a little fender bender, and while you were there at the scene you got a call that some-body'd robbed a convenience store just before the wreck. Didn't take you long to figure that one out."

"But Ruth didn't find any guns this time," Lawton said. "Just that dope."

Hack nodded. "That's right. As in drugs."

A less patient man would just shoot them both, Rhodes thought. But he couldn't do that. It wasn't that he was so patient. It was just that he was sworn to uphold the law, even in the face of the aggravation provided by two old men.

"So Ruth found some drugs," he said. "Where, when, what kind?"

"In a car," Lawton said.

"That was in a wreck," Hack added.

Rhodes took a deep breath, let it out slowly, and said, "I gathered that much. Where in the car and what kind of drugs?"

"Meth," Hack said.

"Ice," Lawton chimed in.

"Crank."

"Speed."

Hack grinned. "Crystal."

"This isn't a synonym game," Rhodes told them.

Hack tried to twist his face into a contrite look and didn't quite make it.

"I guess you're right," he said. "Ruth said the stuff was in plain sight, thanks to the glove box falling open in the crash. It was in a little-bitty plastic bag."

"How much was there?" Rhodes asked.

"Ruth's gonna bring it in. She said maybe a quarter pound."

That would have been worth around two hundred and fifty dollars or so, Rhodes thought, and it was probably cut. Meth dealers would cut the powder with whatever they happened to have, anything from talcum to rat poison to dog-worming pills.

"Did she test it?" Rhodes asked.

"Yep. With that little portable deal y'all carry in the cars. It's the real thing, all right."

"What about the driver?"

"Ruth says he didn't notice at first it was lyin' there, but when he did, he took off runnin', faster than if his hair was on fire."

Rhodes thought about the way amphetamines could affect someone's body chemistry. He thought about how fast the ghost had been running.

"Ruth couldn't go after him," Hack went on, "because there was still somebody in the other car. But she got his license. Name's Burt Trask."

"Never heard of him," Rhodes said.

"He's from out of the county, but it's a good bet he bought the stuff around here. When you catch up with him, you can ask him. That's assumin' you can catch him. From the way Ruth talked, he might be runnin' yet. Heck, he might be in Mexico by now."

"Panama, maybe," Lawton said.

Hack nodded. "Brazil."

"What about an APB?" Rhodes asked.

"Ruth already got me to do that," Hack told him.

"I bet I know just about where Trask got that stuff," Lawton said.

Rhodes didn't take the bet.

"Rapper," he said.

TWENTY

METHAMPHETAMINE HAD never really been a problem in Blacklin County, but Rhodes knew about it, all right. For years, the drug had been made mostly in rural areas because the labs for its manufacture created a powerful smell that was a dead giveaway. Meth labs were easy to find in cities, but in the open country, it was a different matter. They were easy to find if you got close to them, but first you had to get close.

The smell wasn't the only drawback. The manufacturing process also created large amounts of toxic waste. In a city it could be poured into the storm drains and sewers, but that could also lead to getting caught. In the country, you could put it in fifty-five-gallon drums and stack them in a barn.

The fumes that resulted from cooking the meth could be poisonous. More than one meth lab had been shut down not because it was discovered by the law but because the amateur chemists inside it had all died from inhaling their product. It was easier to get good ventilation in the country.

And besides the smell, the toxic waste, and the fumes, there was something else: the labs had a tendency to blow up. City cops noticed things like explosions, even if they occurred in a supposedly abandoned warehouse.

All in all, the country was the best place to run a meth lab, but nowhere was safe. Blacklin County hadn't had any large-scale labs, but meth was getting easier to make, which was a problem for cities, and also for places like Clearview.

Enterprising drug entrepreneurs had rediscovered what was being called the "Nazi cook," a method of making amphetamines that had originated shortly before the beginning of the Second World War, with German scientists who'd been looking for a stimulant that soldiers could cook up themselves while out in the field.

The Nazi cook didn't produce nearly as much meth in one batch as the other method, but it wasn't nearly as dangerous, either. You could find the recipe if you had the time to search the Internet, and you could buy all the ingredients at your friendly neighborhood Wal-Mart. You could make up a small batch in coffee cups if you wanted to, and you could do it in a couple of hours. Less, if you knew what you were doing.

The old labs had required an organization, but they could turn out around a hundred and fifty pounds of the drug in one cooking.

The Nazi method required next to no organization at all. One person could do it. Two people like Rapper and Nellie could make a lot of money at it, even if they got only two pounds from a cooking. They could cut that two pounds to make it ten pounds and get ten thousand dollars for it. Maybe more, if they sold it in small lots.

Rhodes didn't have any doubt at all that the two bikers were in Blacklin County to sell drugs, and he figured that their drug of choice this time was methamphetamine.

Proving it, however, wouldn't be easy, thanks to the absence of fumes and toxic waste in the Nazi cook method. Rhodes couldn't arrest someone for possession of lithium batteries, Styrofoam cups, or any of the other necessary ingredients. He'd have to catch them in the process of cooking the drugs.

"I'm going home and have some supper," he told Hack. "Give me a call if Trask is arrested."

"I'll do that," Hack said.

RHODES HATED TO admit it, but he actually liked veggie lasagna. Even the low-fat sauce was good. And mozzarella cheese was naturally low in fat, so there was plenty of it. Rhodes felt very self-righteous, eating food that was good for him and enjoying it. And it made him feel better about having sneaked those Vienna sausages for lunch.

Yancey was lying in wait under Rhodes's chair, hoping that Rhodes would drop something on the floor, but Rhodes was too careful for that. He didn't want Yancey to get used to eating table scraps, not even very small ones.

Rhodes had told Ivy about his day, and she was interested in all of it. She'd met Rapper and Nellie before, so naturally she wanted to hear Rhodes's theories about the drug lab. But what really interested her was the ghost.

"Two people came in the office today and asked me about it," she said. "Did it really look like Ty Berry?"

"I couldn't tell," Rhodes said. "I didn't see it that well."

"Mary West said it told you that it was going to roam the graveyards until you caught whoever it was that was stealing from them."

"I heard it told me it was going to walk the night until I caught Ty's killer."

Ivy smiled. "It's easy to see that you talked to it for a long time."

Rhodes forked in a mouthful of lasagna, chewed it, and said, "I didn't talk to it at all. I barely even saw it, and I sure didn't catch up with it."

"How's your head?" Ivy asked.

"Fine, as long as I don't touch it."

"I don't think it's swollen much. Your hair hides it, but if you had on a hat, it wouldn't be noticeable at all."

"No hats," Rhodes said. "I don't like hats. They cut off the circulation to my brain."

"That wouldn't be good," Ivy said. "Not that you couldn't operate as well as most people even if you didn't have much blood flow to your brain."

"I don't want to risk it."

"I don't blame you," Ivy said.

AFTER SUPPER, they cleaned up the kitchen and went into the living room to see what was on TV.

Nothing, that was what. There had been a time, not too long before, when Rhodes could find something he wanted to watch on the cable channels, but they'd gotten too sophisticated.

They never showed any of the old Italian Hercules movies, for example. Instead, they had a modern Hercules show, in full color, that was just as bad as any of the old movies. But it wasn't the same, since it was bad on purpose and therefore bad in all the wrong ways. Rhodes didn't like it.

They never showed any of the old horror movies, either. Rhodes couldn't remember the last time he'd seen one of Roger Corman's minor efforts.

Rhodes wondered if he could find a rerun of *Murder, She Wrote*. It might be a good idea to pick up some of those crime-fighting tips from Angela Lansbury.

He'd begun surfing through the channels when the telephone rang.

Ivy answered, listened for a second, then said, "He's right here, Hack. Just a second."

She handed the phone to Rhodes.

"You ready for action?" Hack asked.

"Always," Rhodes said, because that was what Hack expected. To tell the truth, Rhodes wasn't ready for anything more than an hour or so of TV watching.

"That's good," Hack told him, "'cause Ruth needs some backup. She's out at the Dugan Cemetery, and she's got those grave robbers cornered."

THE DUGAN CEMETERY was a couple of miles southeast of Thurston, so it took Rhodes a little over twenty minutes to get there. He didn't want to use the light bar and siren to let the grave robbers know he was coming.

Actually, they weren't grave robbers, not in a technical sense, but Rhodes hadn't wanted to take the time to explain that to Hack. Besides, the phrase fit the situation well enough.

According to Hack, Ruth's county car was a quarter of a mile from the cemetery, pulled off on a side road.

"But she'll be down by the graveyard watching the robbers," Hack had said. "She said to let you know there's plenty of trees around, and if you stay off the road nobody'll spot you coming. She'll be behind a tree somewhere. Try not to shoot her."

In his long career as a law officer, Rhodes had shot hardly anyone at all, and he'd never come close to shooting a deputy. But he thanked Hack for the warning.

Ivy was more worried about Rhodes getting shot than about his shooting someone else.

"Remember what happened at that wrecking yard," she had said as he was getting ready to leave.

"That's the first time anyone's ever shot me," Rhodes said, wincing a little at the thought. Now and then his shoulder still twinged.

"He dropped a car on you, too," Ivy reminded him.

"He tried. But he missed."

"Not completely."

Rhodes didn't flinch at the memory, though he felt like doing so. If the car had been aimed just a little better, he might not have been able to walk quite so well. In fact, he might not have been able to walk at all. That was a thought he didn't want to dwell on.

"I don't think anyone at a country cemetery will be dropping a car on me," he said.

"What about shooting?"

"Nobody will be shooting at me," Rhodes said. "They probably don't even have guns."

"Hah," Ivy had said.

Rhodes didn't blame her. They'd have guns, all right. He turned off the car lights and turned down the dirt road that led to the Dugan Cemetery. It had partially dried out from the previous day's rain, but it was still slick. Driving on it in the dark was a chore, and Rhodes had to be careful not to slide off into the bar ditch.

When he came to the side road that Hack had mentioned, Rhodes turned to the right. *Road* was a relative term. It wasn't much better than a cow track. Ruth's car was pulled off to the side about a hundred yards away.

Rhodes parked behind her and got out. He hoped the cars wouldn't be sunk to the hubs in mud by the time he and Ruth got back to them.

The night was crisp and clear, with plenty of stars against the black sky. Light pollution was creeping down from Dallas, but the sky in Blacklin County still got darker at night than it did in a lot of places these days.

Rhodes took his shotgun from the car and carried it over to a barbed-wire fence. He leaned the gun against a post on the opposite side of the fence, spread the wire, and climbed through. He took the gun and made his way through the trees, hoping he'd find Ruth before he got to the cemetery.

He found her without too much trouble. She was standing behind a big oak tree, occasionally taking a look around the trunk at what was happening in the cemetery.

Rhodes cleared his throat and whispered, "It's me."

Ruth turned around quietly with her pistol leveled at him in a two-handed grip. She lowered it immediately and motioned for him to come up beside her.

Rhodes didn't have to worry about making noise. The people in the cemetery were making enough of their own to cover any stray sounds coming from the trees. But he tried to stay behind cover as best he could.

There appeared to be three people working in the cemetery, and they'd cut the chain on the gates so they could back their big Dodge Ram four-door pick-up inside the wrought-iron fence and load it up.

"They hadn't hit this place before," Ruth said. "I've been watching it pretty closely just in case they thought it was time, and I guess it was."

"How long have they been here?"

"I spotted them a little over half an hour ago. They'd just gotten backed inside. They work pretty fast, though, and I think they're about done."

Rhodes could see several small headstones, probably among the oldest ones, already in the back of the truck. He couldn't tell what else might be in there.

"So what do we do next?" Ruth asked.

"Arrest them," Rhodes said.

He stepped out from behind the tree. A spotlight beam hit him in the face, and then the shooting started.

TWENTY-ONE

RHODES HADN'T SEEN the fourth person in the cemetery, the one who had been sitting inside the pickup, the one who'd apparently been watching him and who'd started firing what sounded like a 9mm pistol in his direction.

When the first shots were fired, the three men who'd been working in the rear of the pickup jumped to the ground. All three of them came up with weapons from somewhere or other. They'd obviously had them close at hand.

And not just any weapons, either. They were as well equipped as a modern army. Rhodes couldn't say exactly what they were shooting, but bullets sprayed everywhere. They clipped leaves off the trees, broke off small limbs, knocked bark off the tree trunks, and sent big chunks of dirt flying all around. Rhodes could hear brass shell casings clinking off tombstones and the side of the truck. The strobing muzzle flashes made the cemetery look like some kind of gothic discotheque.

Rhodes didn't take the time to admire the effects. He was sitting down behind the oak tree with his back to the trunk, holding the shotgun with both hands and telling himself that it was only his imagination that the bullets smacking into the tree trunk were actually jarring it.

Ruth Grady was sitting beside him with her short-barreled .38 in her hand.

"I think I'll let you make the arrest," she said, shouting to make herself heard. "It'll look better in the papers."

"Why don't you make the arrest," Rhodes said, "and I'll take the credit? That's the way the bad sheriffs do things in the movies."

"Too bad you're not that kind of sheriff."

"Yeah," Rhodes said. "It is."

As suddenly as it had started, the shooting stopped. Rhodes didn't waste a second. He rolled to his left and began firing the shotgun. It was essentially a short-range weapon, but the pellets would carry far enough to worry the robbers. There was a sound like hail as the shotgun pellets hit the pickup, and a tinkling crash when the spotlight shattered.

Ruth rolled out on the other side of the tree and triggered off three quick shots from her pistol. Two of them hit the Dodge with a twang of punctured sheet metal.

By that time, the robbers had slapped in fresh clips, and the graveyard lit up again. Rhodes and Ruth rolled back behind the tree.

"Good shooting," Ruth said. She reloaded her pistol. "I don't think I could have hit that light even with a shotgun."

Adrenaline was jangling through Rhodes's veins like electricity. Hitting the spotlight had been nothing more than luck. In fact, Rhodes thought he was lucky just to hold his hands steady, but he didn't see any need to tell Ruth that.

He said, "I go to the range and practice a lot."

"I'll bet you do. They're going to make a run for it, you know."

"Figures," Rhodes said.

"Either that or they'll kill us."

"You're a real comfort," Rhodes said.

He shoved three shells into the shotgun, pulled his

Chief's Special from the holster at his back and waited for the fusillade to end.

When it did, he rolled to his right and stood up. Sure enough, the three men were getting in the truck. Rhodes didn't try to shoot them. He aimed for the truck tires, hoping he'd get lucky again and not disgrace himself.

Ruth was on the other side of the tree, and she was also firing at the tires.

Rhodes hit a rear tire with his second shot. It exploded, and the back of the truck sank to the right.

It took Ruth three shots to get the other back tire and level the truck's rear end. Rhodes got a front tire just before the men slapped in some more clips and fired back.

Behind the tree again, Rhodes said, "How much ammunition do you think they have?"

"Probably not much more than the Russian army," Ruth said as she reloaded. "I hear they've fallen on hard times. The Russians, I mean."

Rhodes closed the cylinder of his pistol. "Whatever they have, it's more than we do. And their firepower's a little more advanced than ours, too."

"Maybe so, but we have them right where we want them. They'll never be able to drive that truck out of there with those flat tires."

"I wouldn't be too sure of that," Rhodes said.

He heard the sound of the Dodge's engine over a lull in the firing. He rolled again.

They'd left one man with a rifle outside the truck to protect their backs, but Rhodes ignored the bullets whizzing over his head and popped off a couple of shots at the truck, which was lugging forward toward the gates.

One bullet spiderwebbed a hole through the back glass, and the truck stopped suddenly, as did the shooting.

Rhodes stood up.

"Shotgun," he said, and Ruth tossed it to him. He caught it in his left hand and holstered his pistol. He ran toward the cemetery with Ruth at his side and a little behind.

Three of the robbers abandoned the truck and headed through the gates for the trees.

Rhodes knew it wouldn't do any good for him to yell for them to stop, but he did it anyway. It had exactly the effect he thought it would.

"Check out the truck," he said to Ruth as they came to the fence.

She was a lot younger than Rhodes, and she wasn't puffing at all from the short run. Rhodes was. He thought she might vault right over the fence, but he was glad to see she headed for the gates.

"I'll see if I can catch up with any of them," he said.

He had to pause in the middle to take a breath, but he didn't think Ruth noticed.

There wasn't much doubt that the three runners would split up. Rhodes could hear them thrashing through the trees. He decided to go after the one in the middle, who seemed to be making a bit more noise than the others. Maybe that meant he was a little clumsier.

When he heard a shot from the direction of the graveyard, he came to an abrupt halt, his feet slipping in the mud and wet leaves.

Ruth was in trouble. Rhodes could go on and hope she came out of things all right, or he could go back, in which case the runners would certainly get away. He didn't have any difficulty making a decision. He turned around.

It was too dark to see much, but Rhodes could see enough. There was a fourth runner now, and Rhodes watched as he vaulted the fence easily, heading in the direction opposite that taken by his cohorts.

Ruth was sitting on the ground by the Dodge Ram, shooting at the fleeing figure. Rhodes ran around the edge of the fence, hoping Ruth would recognize him and not shoot. He didn't have enough wind to tell her who he was.

The man ahead of him was listing slightly to the left and holding a rifle in his right hand. That was all Rhodes could tell, and then he lost sight of him. He could hear him, however, so he kept following.

He had gone for about a quarter of a mile before the noises stopped. When they did, so did Rhodes.

He stood there sweating and trying not to pant too loudly. His blood was pounding in his head, but he took deep breaths, and eventually his pulse slowed.

Gradually he began to hear a few quiet sounds, the scratching of leaves over his head, a squirrel skittering through the branches of a nearby tree. But there was nothing from the man he'd been chasing. He'd obviously gone to ground somewhere not too far away.

As Rhodes stood there, it dawned on him that he'd most likely made a big mistake. Maybe two or three of them.

To begin with, he'd let someone lure him off into the woods. And in doing so, he'd left Ruth back there alone. What was to keep the three grave robbers from turning around and coming back to attack her? Rhodes couldn't think of a thing.

To make things worse, for all Rhodes knew, the man he'd been after might be standing behind the trunk of the next tree, ready to riddle Rhodes with bullets or, if he was out of bullets, to crack Rhodes's skull with his rifle butt.

That was the trouble with leading a quiet life, Rhodes thought. When it came time for action, you didn't have experience to guide you. So you reacted to the situation without thinking it through. You let an adrenaline rush dictate your actions.

He'd known that he wasn't going to be able to walk out from behind that tree and say, "Hands up!" and get the right response, but he'd done it anyway—and had gotten the wrong response. And then he'd let himself be led away from the crime scene and into the dark woods.

Of course the robbers might not be as clever as he thought they were. It could be that they were simply working by instinct, too.

But he didn't think so. It was all too well orchestrated, almost as if they'd practiced it.

Rhodes peered into the darkness. He saw trees and bushes and nothing else. He didn't hear anything, either. Even the squirrel was quiet.

Rhodes wasn't going to walk into a trap, not if he could help it. He turned and headed back to the cemetery.

And walked right into a trap.

TWENTY-TWO

THE THREE OF THEM had turned back, all right, but Rhodes didn't see them at first. He just saw Ruth Grady sitting on the ground, leaning against a tombstone.

She raised a hand to warn him, but it was too late. A man stepped around the pickup and trained a rifle on Rhodes. He was lean as a hoe handle and wore jeans, a black T-shirt, and a Texas Rangers cap. He had the bottom half of the T-shirt pulled up over his mouth and nose, while the bill of the cap obscured the upper part of his face. His stomach was revealed, flat and hard, but Rhodes didn't think it was going to help him to identify the man later on.

"You can just stop right there, Sheriff," he said. "We don't want to have to shoot you."

Rhodes didn't particularly want them to have to shoot him, either, so he said, "What *do* you want?"

"We just want to drive out of here and be left alone. Jack the shells out of that shotgun."

Rhodes worked the pump action until all the shells were lying on the ground around him.

"Now put the gun on the ground," the man ordered, and when Rhodes had obeyed, he said, "And now the pistol. Dump the bullets first."

Rhodes opened the cylinder and let the cartridges drop on the ground.

"Okay," the man said. "Drop it."

Rhodes did.

"I bet you got some handcuffs on you," the man said. "Probably those nice new plastic ones."

Rhodes didn't say anything. The man motioned to someone in the shadows, and a woman came out from in front of the truck. She was dressed just like the man and had pulled up her T-shirt to cover her face. Her navel was pierced by a small gold ring, and she was carrying what looked to Rhodes like a Glock automatic pistol.

"Get the cuffs," the man told her.

Instead of going to Rhodes, the woman went to Ruth and stuck the gun to her head while she removed the cuffs from the pouch that held them.

Each cuff consisted of a single strand of tough plastic about a half inch wide. One end was pulled tight through an opening on the other and locked automatically. The cuffs were much easier to use than traditional steel cuffs, and they were even harder to remove. There was no key; they had to be cut.

"Let me do that," said a man behind Rhodes.

It was the one Rhodes had followed. He came up beside Ruth, and the woman backed away, still aiming her pistol at Ruth.

The man took the cuffs and said, "Put your hands behind you."

Ruth looked at Rhodes, who nodded. She put her hands behind her back, and the man looped the strand of plastic around her wrists and pulled it tight.

He turned to face Rhodes. He hadn't bothered to cover his face, but then he didn't have to. He had a bushy black beard that hadn't been trimmed in years, and his hair was so bushy that the baseball cap he wore was almost obscured by it. All he had to do was get a haircut and shave, and no one would be able to recognize him.

He did, however, have a distinguishing mark. He'd

been wounded in the shoulder, most likely by the shot Rhodes had fired through the pickup's back glass. There was a good bit of blood on his T-shirt. The wound didn't seem to be bothering him at all, however, and it certainly hadn't impaired his movement.

"Your turn," he told Rhodes.

Rhodes let himself be cuffed. When the man was satisfied, he said, "Sit over there by the deputy."

Rhodes didn't like being ordered around, but they had the guns, so he did as he was told.

"Let's go," the first man said.

"Can't," the man holding the rifle on Rhodes and Ruth said. "Damn tires are all flat."

"Truck'll run. These two won't be following us for a while. Get in."

"Let me pick up these guns first," the bearded man said.

He took Rhodes's pistol and the shotgun. Rhodes assumed that they had Ruth's pistol already.

When he had the guns, the man went to the truck. When he got there, the two men and the woman got in the truck along with a fourth man that Rhodes caught only a glimpse of. He'd obscured his face like the other man, so the look didn't help Rhodes at all.

The pickup started and moved sluggishly out through the cemetery gates.

"What a revoltin' development this is," Rhodes said as he watched the red taillights slowly move away.

"It's not so bad," Ruth said. "We got fooled, but we're alive."

"What happened when you checked the truck?"

"That man who came up at the last there was slumped over the wheel. There was a lot of blood, and I thought he might be dead. He wasn't. When I got close to the door, he slammed it into me and knocked me down. Then he took off for the tall timber."

"And I was dumb enough to go after him," Rhodes said.

"Let's don't talk about being dumb," Ruth said. "Especially since I'm the one who watched you running after him and just stood there while those other three came up and stuck a gun in my back. They made me sit here until you got back."

"What would they have done if I hadn't come?"

"I don't know. Do you think they had it figured that far ahead?"

"Looks that way to me. Let's see if we can get to the cars and get out of these cuffs."

"We won't have to go that far," Ruth said. "There's a cuff cutter in a holster on the back of my belt."

She and Rhodes turned until they had their backs to each other, and Rhodes managed to fumble the cutter out of the holster. His fingers were getting numb. He dropped the cutter almost as soon as he had it, but he groped around until he had it again. Working by guess and by God, he finally got the jaws open and then closed them on the plastic strand around Ruth's wrists. Or what he hoped was the plastic.

"Is that right?" he asked.

"I think so. Give it a try."

Rhodes mashed the handles together, met resistance, and mashed harder. The plastic parted.

Rhodes dropped the cutter. Ruth flexed her fingers and then picked up the cutter and freed Rhodes.

They both stood up. Rhodes's fingers stung and tingled as the circulation began to return to them. The bearded man had pulled the cuff a lot tighter than was necessary.

"Ought to be easy to follow them," Ruth said. "They can't be going too fast with those tires."

"You'd probably be surprised," Rhodes said.

"Too bad they had their faces covered. How are we going to identify them?"

"Navel ring?" Rhodes said.

"Everybody has one of those."

Rhodes gave her a quizzical look.

"Not me. I didn't mean *every*body. Just a lot of people."

"Right. Well, maybe we don't have to worry about their faces."

"The license plate was smeared with mud," Ruth said. "I noticed."

"So did I. But I could read parts of three of the numbers. Enough to tell what they were, I think. That should do it."

"Are you sure?"

"No. But Hack keeps telling me about the wonders of computers. If they can't figure out which Dodge Ram has those three numbers, then they're not nearly as good as he thinks they are."

"I guess you could find out."

"I guess I could," Rhodes said. "I'll go to the car, and you can look around here to see if there's anything that'll help us. Collect some of that brass."

There were bullet casings all over the ground. It was as if a small war had been fought there, which it had, in a way.

"I'll be back with a flashlight," Rhodes said. "Don't step on anything important."

"I'll be careful," Ruth said.

As soon as he got back to the county cars, Rhodes called Hack on the radio.

"I need a make on a license plate," he said.

"Gimme the numbers," Hack said.

Rhodes gave him what he had.

"That ain't gonna get it."

"You mean to tell me a computer can't work it out?"

"It might, at that. Let me get to the DPS. You hang on."

Rhodes told him that he couldn't do much else. While he was waiting for Hack to talk to the Department of Public Safety, he located the flashlight and some evidence bags.

In only a few minutes, Hack was back on the radio again.

"I bet I got it," he said. "I asked 'em if they had reports of stolen plates. Turns out they do, so I got 'em to check those first. There was a set of plates with those numbers stolen over in the next county about a month ago."

"So they didn't belong on a Dodge Ram," Rhodes said.

"Nope. On a Ford Ranger. So where does that leave you?"

"We'll start checking out the Dodge Ram owners tomorrow. Right now, I have a crime scene to investigate. Maybe I'll find a clue."

"That'd be nice."

"Wouldn't it, though," Rhodes said.

TWENTY-THREE

RHODES DROVE BACK TO the cemetery, where Ruth had found something interesting. He got out of the car and walked over to where she was holding it up for him to examine. It was a night-vision scope with a little lever on top, and Ruth was holding it with her fingertips on the edges of the lever.

"You squeeze the lever for power," Ruth said. "No batteries to get low."

"So they probably saw me when I stood up," Rhodes said.

"It was the woman," Ruth told him. "She was the one in the cab, and it must've fallen out in the confusion. She was scoping the woods while the men did the heavy work."

"Sexists," Rhodes said, handing her an evidence bag.

"You get a lot of that in your criminal classes." Ruth took the bag and put the scope inside it. "Fingerprints would be better than trying to identify that navel ring. Did you get anything from Hack?"

Rhodes told her about the license plate.

"Are you sure that's the right one?"

"No, but it's a good bet that it is. Our friends seem like the kind of people who'd steal a license plate. Did you find anything besides the scope and the brass?"

"Not a thing. We can try with the flashlight, and I can come back tomorrow if I need to."

They went about it methodically, but they didn't find anything more.

"I might have an idea about who those people were," Ruth said after about fifteen minutes. "If you want to hear it."

"Any idea at all would help," Rhodes said. "What have you got?"

"The Packers," Ruth said.

Rhodes had had plenty of dealings with the Packers over the years, though he wasn't sure exactly how many of them were Packers, since they had an extreme disdain for all civil and religious ceremonies, including marriage. Maybe especially marriage.

He didn't know exactly how many of them there were, either. They all lived together in the country out around the little town of Obert, where they did pretty much what they pleased. They hunted out of season and trespassed on other people's land to do it. They fished in every stock tank within a five-mile radius of where they lived. They stole corn and watermelons from the fields. As far as Rhodes knew, none of them worked at a regular job. Several of them had been in and out of the county jail at one time or another for a variety of misdemeanors, minor and otherwise, and the occasional felony.

In another century, the Packers might have been called outlaws, though that wouldn't have been a strictly accurate description. It was true that they lived outside the law, but it was their attitude as much as their actions that defined them. As far as they were concerned, the law just didn't matter. They were simply indifferent to it.

"Did you recognize any of them?" he asked.

"No," Ruth said, "but it's their style, isn't it? And robbing graveyards is just the kind of thing they'd do. They wouldn't see a thing wrong with it. In fact, they'd probably resent it if you told them it was against the law.''

Rhodes thought she was right. The Packers would regard the idea of dead people having any rights as ridiculous, and they wouldn't see how stealing from cemeteries could affect the living. Not that they would have cared if it did.

"I guess we should check and see if any of that bunch owns a new Dodge pickup," he said. "We can do that tomorrow. Let's look around here for a little longer before we give up. You might want to come back in the morning to check it out during the daylight."

"They really made a mess, didn't they?" Ruth said.

"They certainly did, and they hauled off half the stones in the cemetery. Maybe this time we'll get them back."

"Where do you think they got all those guns?" Ruth asked.

"Probably at a flea market or a gun show. They aren't that hard to get. If anyone can get them, the Packers can. Are you turning into a gun-control advocate?"

"I wasn't thinking of that. I was thinking that they could have killed us."

"I don't think so," Rhodes told her. He'd been thinking about the same thing. "I believe they just wanted to scare us away. If they'd wanted to kill us, it would have been easy enough. They don't mind stealing, or any of the other things they do, but they've never killed anybody. At least that we know about."

"What about Ty Berry?"

"I'm not sure about Ty. But even if they did kill him, we're different. We're law officers. If they'd killed us, they'd have to leave the state. Or the country. They'd have every sheriff, local cop, DPS officer, and Texas

Ranger in the state after them. They wouldn't want to kill us. We'd cause them a lot more trouble dead than we've ever caused them while we're alive.''

"That's a comforting thought," Ruth said. "I guess."

"It's the best I can do," Rhodes said.

RHODES GOT IN LATE and gave Ivy only a sketchy idea of what had happened. He confessed that there had been a few shots fired, but he didn't say how many. And he didn't mention the handcuffs.

He was up early the next morning, but by the time he got to the jail, Hack already had some information for him.

"I checked the courthouse records. Runt Packer bought a Dodge Ram about five months ago."

Runt's real name was Samuel, and he hadn't gotten his nickname because of his current size. In fact, as Rhodes recalled, Runt was about four inches over six feet tall and almost as wide. But he'd been born prematurely and had weighed around four pounds at birth. He'd been kept in the hospital for several weeks, and his family had called him Runt forever after. It might have been his Dodge Ram, but he hadn't been one of the four in the cemetery. Rhodes would have recognized him from his size alone.

"I guess I'll have to pay the Packers a little visit, then," Rhodes said.

"You better have some backup, considering what went down last night," Hack said.

"Who told you about that?"

"I talked to Ruth. She said there was lots of shootin' goin' on."

"Don't spread that around. Ivy thinks there were one or two shots fired, but that's it."

"What about the paper? Ruth wrote up a report. Somebody'll read it sooner or later."

The Clearview *Herald* sent someone over about once a week to go through the records. Then the most colorful crimes would find their way into the paper.

"Maybe she won't read it," Rhodes said.

Hack snorted.

"I'll tell her the paper exaggerated," Rhodes said. "She knows that happens."

Hack snorted louder. He was about to say something when the phone rang. He listened for a few seconds before saying, "You're gonna have to go a little slower, Miz Tabor. I can't get anything written down if you're talkin' so fast." He found a pencil and started writing. "Okay, you can go ahead. Yes, that's fine. I'm gettin' it now.... She didn't show up at all? All right. I got it. And you've called her three times this morning.... I got that.... Well, I don't blame you, Miz Tabor. I'd be worried, too.... Yes, ma'am, I'll be sure to tell the sheriff. He's standin' right here. I'll send him right on over there. Don't you worry. I'm sure there's nothin' wrong, but we'll check on it."

Hack hung up the phone and turned to Rhodes. "That was Ida Louise Tabor. Looks like there's a little problem with Faye Knape."

"What problem?" Rhodes asked.

"Seems like she didn't show up for the Chickenfoot game last night," Hack said. "Miz Tabor called her, but she didn't get an answer. Called back twice this morning, too. Still didn't get an answer. I told her you'd get on over there and check things out. Unless you want somebody else to do it."

Rhodes needed to pay a visit to the Packers, but he could go by and see about Faye on his way.

"I'll go," he told Hack. "And while I'm gone, you check and see who owned those buildings."

Hack gave him a hurt look. "I'm already workin' on that," he said.

TWENTY-FOUR

WHEN RHODES STOPPED his car in front of Faye Knape's house, nothing appeared to be wrong or out of place. It was a beautiful day. The sun was shining, there were big fluffy white clouds in the sky, and sparrows were flickering in and out of the trees in Faye's yard.

Rhodes got out of the car and looked down the driveway at the garage. The door was up, and Rhodes could see the rear end of Faye's car, a seven-year-old Pontiac.

"Sheriff Rhodes," someone called. "Are you Sheriff Rhodes?"

Rhodes turned around and saw a woman coming across the street. She was wrapped up in a purple flannel housecoat and wore fuzzy pink slippers. She had a coffee cup in one hand and a cigarette in the other.

"Are you Sheriff Rhodes?" she asked again when she reached him.

"That's me," he said. "How can I help you?"

"I've seen your picture in the paper. I thought I recognized you, but I wanted to be sure. I'm Melva Keeler, and I live across the street there."

She pointed with her cigarette, and Rhodes looked over at a dilapidated frame house that didn't appear to have been painted since his Edsel was new.

And Melva Keeler appeared to have been living there at least that long and probably longer. She had untidy gray hair that she had carelessly pinned up on her head and wore no makeup to cover the dark circles under her eyes.

She took a drag on her cigarette and said, "I should have called you yesterday, but I didn't really think it was necessary. Now I'm not so sure."

"Why not?" Rhodes asked.

"Because every morning, Faye comes out and gets her newspaper about the same time I do. We always say something, you know, 'Good morning,' or whatever. But not today. Look."

She pointed with her cigarette again, this time at the *Dallas Morning News* that lay on the sidewalk not far from where they were standing.

"You mentioned something about yesterday," Rhodes said.

"It was awful," Melva said. "I was sitting on the porch reading a book when it happened."

"What happened?"

"It was really a coincidence, since the book I was reading was *Wild Texas Wind*. Do you believe in coincidences, Sheriff?"

"Not usually."

"Neither do I, but I guess that's what you'd have to call it. There I was, sitting on the porch and reading that book, when who should drive up but Vernell Lindsey. Did you know she wrote a book?"

Rhodes said that he knew.

Melva took a sip of coffee and a drag from her cigarette. The cigarette was smoked down almost to the filter, and she dropped it to the sidewalk and stepped on it with one of the fuzzy slippers. Rhodes thought briefly about asking her if she was aware of the local littering laws but decided it wouldn't do any good.

"I think it's just wonderful that someone from Clearview has the talent to write a book," Melva said. "Don't you?"

"Sure. And you say Vernell was here yesterday?"

"That's right, and I could tell as soon as she got out of the car that she was hopping mad. She slammed the door and practically ran up to Faye's porch."

Rhodes had a bad feeling about where this conversation was heading, and he wondered if he might have been responsible in some way. But he was sure he hadn't mentioned any names to Vernell Lindsey.

"Faye came to the door," Melva went on, "and Vernell just started right in on her, yelling real loud. You can guess how much Faye liked that."

Rhodes's guess would have been that Faye didn't like it at all, but Melva didn't give him a chance to say so.

"Faye got red in the face and started yelling right back at her. I was afraid they were both going to have strokes right there on Faye's front porch."

Melva paused and looked into her coffee cup. It was nearly empty, and she turned it upside down to pour the last couple of drops out on the sidewalk.

"Could you hear what they were saying?" Rhodes asked.

Melva looked down at the two dark spots on the walk and said, "No. They were yelling, but they were too far away to hear. And then they went inside."

"How long were they in there?"

"It must have been fifteen minutes. I managed to get quite a few pages of the book read, but I'm a very fast reader. When Vernell came out, I walked to the front of the porch and waved to her. I wanted to tell her how much I was enjoying her book. I thought that if she was a little out of sorts, a compliment might help. I've found that compliments often do."

She looked at Rhodes as if expecting some kind of

compliment from him. He didn't know what to say, since he wasn't all that fond of fuzzy pink slippers.

"Did it help?" he asked.

"I didn't get a chance to say anything. She just jumped in her car and tore out of here like a bat. You know the kind of bat I mean?"

Rhodes said that he knew.

"And now Faye hasn't come out for her newspaper. She's never let it stay there that long, not even when she had the flu last fall. I should have called you yesterday."

"Maybe she's just sleeping late," Rhodes said. "I'll check."

"All right," Melva said.

Rhodes went up to the porch. Before he knocked on the door, he looked back, and Melva was still standing there in her robe and fuzzy slippers, watching him. He wished she'd go back to her own house, but he didn't feel like telling her that.

He looked around the porch. It was very quiet, and there were no cats in the windows. A sparrow fluttered in a nearby tree. Rhodes knocked.

There was no answer, but then he hadn't really been expecting one. He tried the doorknob, which turned easily in his hand. The door wasn't locked.

He opened it and went inside and called Faye's name. His voice echoed off the hardwood floors and bounced down the walls of the hallway.

There was no sign of the cats, but Rhodes knew they were there somewhere. He could feel his eyes beginning to itch already.

He walked down the short hall to the living room. Faye Knape was lying on the floor, her knees drawn up, her mouth open as if in a scream. Her forehead had been crushed. The cut-glass vase lay not faraway, and the dried flowers were scattered on the floor.

TWENTY-FIVE

RHODES FORGOT ABOUT his eyes and looked around the living room. Nothing other than the vase seemed to be out of place; aside from that, the room looked exactly as he'd left it.

He turned and went back outside, where Melva Keeler was still standing on the walk. She watched him coming toward her with wide eyes.

"Is Faye...all right?" she asked.

"No," Rhodes said. "She's not. Do you know what time it was when Vernell Lindsey came by yesterday?"

Melva's eyes went vague. Then they cleared and she said, "There was still enough light to read by, but it was already getting late. It must have been around four-thirty. Maybe a little later. Should I go call an ambulance?"

"I'll take care of that," Rhodes said. "There's no hurry."

"You mean that Faye is...dead?"

"That's right. Do you remember whether anyone else came by after Vernell left?"

"I went inside right after she left. It was getting a little chilly. And then I watched the news and ate supper. After that I watched a rerun of *Murder, She Wrote*. I just love Jessica Fletcher. Faye does, too. Sometimes we'd talk about the show when we picked up our newspapers."

Her eyes filled with tears, and she brushed them with the sleeve of her robe.

"I guess I won't be talking to her about anything anymore." She paused. "Did she have a stroke?"

"I don't think so," Rhodes said, wishing it was as simple as that.

"What was it, then?"

"I'm not sure."

"Did Vernell…do something?"

"I'm not sure about that, either."

"Oh, dear," Melva said, and then her face changed as another thought struck her. "Who's going to take care of Faye's boys?"

"The boys?" Rhodes said, but then he remembered. "You mean the cats?"

"Yes. Someone will have to take care of them. Faye treated them just like members of her family. And someone has to feed them right now. They're probably starving, and I'm sure they wonder what's happened to her."

"I'll feed them," Rhodes said.

"But who's going to take care of them after that?"

Not me, Rhodes thought. He said, "I don't know."

RHODES CALLED HACK and said that he wouldn't be going out to see the Packers for a while. He asked him to send Buddy Reynolds to Vernell Lindsey's house.

"Somethin' wrong?" Hack asked.

"You could say that," Rhodes told him. "Faye's dead. Looks like somebody killed her."

"That's bad, all right. Faye was a little gripey, but she was okay. I'll get Buddy out to Vernell's. What's he supposed to do there?"

Rhodes thought it over. "Send him by here instead. I'll talk to Vernell myself."

"All right. 'Fore I let you go, though, there's somethin' you need to know."

"What's that?"

"You remember those buildings you wanted me to check on?"

Rhodes had to admit that the buildings had slipped his mind. Finding Faye like that had pushed everything else right out of his head.

"What about them?" he asked.

"Well, I guess you could say it's a kind of a coincidence, you wantin' me to find out who owned 'em and all."

There were getting to be too many coincidences, Rhodes thought.

"What kind of coincidence?" he asked.

"The kind where it turns out that they were owned by Faye Knape," Hack said.

Hack went on to explain that Faye hadn't bought them or anything like that. They'd been left to her by her husband at his death. He'd owned them under a corporate name, the Wendigo Corporation, of which Faye had been the vice president and treasurer.

"It was easy to check on," Hack had said. "Since there'd already been somebody going through the records. Mary Cate works with that stuff in the courthouse, and she knew all about it. And guess who was the one that'd been checking it all out?"

Rhodes knew the answer to that one. Vernell Lindsey had told him.

"Ty Berry," he said.

"Right the first time. What d'you think it all means?"

"I don't have any idea," Rhodes said.

HE THOUGHT ABOUT IT while he leaned against the county car and waited for Buddy Reynolds to arrive. Ty had been mighty upset about the buildings, and, according to Vernell, he might even have been considering a lawsuit against the owners for negligence or whatever other charges a good lawyer could come up with. Rhodes was sure there were any number of things even a mediocre lawyer could think of if there was a chance of getting some money out of the deal.

Had Ty told Faye that he knew she owned the buildings? If he had, that was plenty of motive for her to kill him right there. The lawsuit would have ruined her personally even if it hadn't affected her financially. It would have destroyed her credibility with the Historical Society, and that would have been far worse from Faye's point of view than losing every penny she had in the bank.

But if Faye had killed Ty, who had killed Faye? Vernell Lindsey?

Right now it looked as if Vernell were the culprit, all right, which was too bad. Rhodes liked Vernell in spite of her bad temper, and he thought it would be a shame for her to go to prison just as she'd finally achieved her life's ambition and published a novel. On the other hand, maybe she could use jail time to write a book about women in prison. Rhodes thought about a bad movie he'd seen once. *Chained Heat.* Somehow he couldn't see Vernell in it. She wasn't the Sybil Danning type.

He couldn't see Vernell as a killer, either, no matter how much it appeared that she might be. Rhodes knew better than to rule someone out merely because of his own feelings, however. He'd been wrong before.

At that point, Buddy Reynolds pulled up and got out of the county car. Buddy was thin, with a narrow face, narrow shoulders, and a narrow mind. He didn't approve of smoking, drinking, or public displays of affection. If it had been up to him, all three would have been classified as felony crimes. But the thing Rhodes liked best about him was that he didn't let his narrowness interfere with the way he did his job.

"Hack tells me you got a problem," Buddy said, squinting in the morning sun. He squinted in the evenings, too.

"It's Faye Knape," Rhodes told him. "Somebody's killed her."

Buddy's eyes narrowed even further. "You know who it was yet?"

"Nope. That's where you come in. I want you to talk to all the neighbors, except for Melva Keeler. She lives right across the street, and I've already talked to her. I want you to find out if they saw anybody visit Faye's house yesterday afternoon or evening, from around four o'clock on. After you've done that, you go see Ida Louise Tabor and ask about last night's Chickenfoot game. Faye was supposed to be there, but she wasn't. Ida Louise says she called her. Find out when she called and how many times she called. Ask if anybody in the group drove by to check on Faye. If somebody did, find out who it was."

Rhodes paused to give Buddy a chance to ask questions, but Buddy only looked at him.

"When you've got all that taken care of, go back to the jail and write up a report for me. I'll get by there and read it later. Or if I'm still here, you can just tell me."

"What're you gonna do here?" Buddy asked.

"Search the house," Rhodes said.

BEFORE HE SEARCHED, Rhodes fed the cats. The house had a small enclosed back porch, just large enough for a washing machine, a dryer, and six cat bowls, three of which held water and three of which were for dry cat food. There was a bag of the dry food in a cabinet over the washer, so Rhodes got it down and put some in each of the bowls.

One of the cats came out of hiding when he heard the sound and poked his head around the edge of the doorframe. It was a big gray tabby, and when he saw Rhodes, he disappeared. Neither of the others showed up. Rhodes figured they were still under a bed somewhere. He put the food sack back in the cabinet and looked at the water bowls. They were all about half full, but Rhodes decided that the cats would like it better if it was fresh, so he refilled the bowls in the kitchen. When he was finished, he sneezed twice. His eyes were itching furiously, but he didn't rub them. Resisting the urge, he went to look at the rest of the house.

First, he took another look at the living room and Faye's body. He'd brought the Polaroid camera from the county car, and he took some photos to show the position of the body relative to the vase, though he didn't think they'd prove useful, especially the two he'd taken when he was sneezing. The vase, if it had been smooth, might have provided some fingerprints, but it was cut glass, all pointy rough edges that wouldn't be any help at all.

When he was finished taking pictures and looking over the room, Rhodes called Clyde Ballinger and told him what had happened. Ballinger said that he'd be there shortly, and Rhodes went to get some tissues from the box on the end table. He sneezed a couple of times and moved on to the rest of the house to see what he could find.

He located two of the cats, one of whom was in a closet with a half-open door. He came streaking out when Rhodes opened the door all the way, and Rhodes didn't see him again.

There was nothing out of the ordinary in any of the

rooms except for the back bedroom that Faye Knape was using for an office. In one corner of the room there was an unlocked gun cabinet. Rhodes remembered that Faye had mentioned selling her late husband's guns, and when he opened the doors on the cabinet, it was empty. There were places where pistols had been mounted and where rifles and a double-barreled shotgun had stood. The inside was free of dust, as if Faye had recently cleaned it.

There was a computer on a desk in the middle of the room, but Rhodes didn't find anything helpful on the computer's hard drive or on any of the disks that Faye had filed neatly away in a plastic box.

What he did find was in a drawer in the computer desk, one that slid open easily when he pulled it, as if it had been recently oiled.

Looking inside, Rhodes saw a new ink cartridge for the printer, an instruction manual for the scanner, and a couple of blank disks. Rhodes wasn't surprised to see them.

What he was surprised to see was the small two-shot .22 derringer that lay half hidden under a blank white memo pad.

TWENTY-SIX

RHODES PICKED UP the gun with his fingertips and sniffed it. It had been fired fairly recently, probably within the last couple of days. So what did that mean? One answer, certainly the most obvious, was that Faye had killed Ty Berry and that Rhodes was holding the murder weapon in his hand. He put it in an evidence bag and marked the bag carefully. He didn't want any mistakes.

He was putting the bag in his car when Clyde Ballinger arrived, along with his two helpers.

"This is pretty bad, Sheriff," Ballinger said. "Two outstanding citizens dead within a couple of days. What's Clearview coming to?"

Rhodes said that he didn't know.

"Was she shot, like Ty?"

"No. Somebody hit her with something, probably a flower vase."

"Any idea who did it?"

"You know better than to ask me that," Rhodes said.

"Sure, but you never know when I'll sneak one by you. This is going to have the county commissioners in an uproar, you know."

Rhodes nodded. He wasn't worried about the commissioners. They liked to have everything solved neatly and quickly, but things didn't always work out that way.

"The paper's going to be all over it, too," Ballinger said. "I mean, we've lost the president of both the county's historical associations. This is big news, like there's some kind of weird serial killer on the loose. If

Ed McBain were telling the story, the Deaf Man would be behind it.''

Ballinger liked to read paperback books about cops and killers, and he always seemed to enjoy comparing Rhodes's cases to something he'd read about. McBain was one of his particular favorites.

"You mean the 'hearing impaired' man," Rhodes said.

"No, I mean the Deaf Man. He's a character that turns up now and then to try to outwit the guys in the Eighty-Seventh Precinct. Killing off the presidents of the historical associations, that's something he'd do, since it doesn't seem like it makes any sense. But in the end, it does.''

"I would hope so," Rhodes said.

"Yeah," Ballinger agreed. "And it's the sort of thing the media love. I'll be surprised if some of the Dallas TV channels don't send their reporters down.''

"Let's hope not," Rhodes said.

"Well, you never know. What about Dr. White?''

"Give him a call," Rhodes said.

"All right." Ballinger turned to his helpers, who had been standing silently by. "Let's go see about Mrs. Knape.''

Rhodes watched them go inside. He had the uneasy feeling that there was something in the house that he'd overlooked, but he couldn't imagine what it was. He forgot about it when Buddy Reynolds came sauntering up.

"What did you find out?" Rhodes asked him.

Buddy shook his head disgustedly. "Nobody saw a thing. I thought this was supposed to be a small town, with everybody minding everybody else's business, didn't you?''

Rhodes nodded.

"Well, it's not that way around this neighborhood. According to all Miz Knape's neighbors, they were either gone or inside their houses minding nobody's business but their own. I don't think we're gonna get any help around here."

"Probably not. You go on and talk to Ida Louise Tabor. You can leave me a report at the jail."

Buddy left, and Rhodes saw Ballinger coming out of Faye's house, walking in front of a gurney that held Faye's draped body.

Rhodes got in his car. It was time to visit Vernell Lindsey.

VERNELL'S HOUSE hadn't improved since Rhodes had seen it last. As he walked up to the door, he could hear the goats bleating in the back yard. He hoped they'd stay there.

Vernell came to the door wearing very tight jeans and a Tweety Bird T-shirt. She still wasn't wearing any shoes. Rhodes wondered if she'd been barefoot when she visited Faye Knape.

"What is it this time, Sheriff?" she asked. "I'm right in the middle of a crucial scene."

"It's about Faye Knape," Rhodes said. "Can I come in?"

"That old bat," Vernell said, but she stepped back from the door and held it open for Rhodes.

He went inside, and Vernell closed the door. Then she led him to the den, which was still in disarray.

"I understand you went to see Faye yesterday afternoon," Rhodes said when he was seated.

"Yes, I did. Why are you asking? Did she file some kind of complaint?"

"Not exactly," Rhodes said.

"Well, it's a good thing. She said just as many bad things to me as I did to her."

"What did you say them for?" Rhodes asked.

"You should know the answer to that. She's the one who sent you over here yesterday. She accused me of killing Ty Berry."

Rhodes didn't say anything.

"You don't have to look at me that way," Vernell said. She lit a cigarette. "I know you didn't tell me, but you didn't have to. That meddlesome Faye has never liked me, just because I know as much about history as she does. Probably more. And she was jealous of me because I was going out with Ty. Personally, I think she wanted him for herself."

"I didn't get that impression," Rhodes said.

"Of course not." Vernell exhaled smoke. "She wouldn't have wanted anyone to know. But I think that's why she complained about him so much. If he'd done what she wanted and asked her out, she'd have liked him just fine."

Rhodes thought about that. Could Faye have killed Ty because he rejected her? Add that to the fact that Ty knew she owned the collapsed buildings, and you had a pretty good motive.

"I take it that the two of you argued yesterday," he said.

Vernell knocked some ash off the end of her cigarette into the Texas-shaped ashtray.

"You could say that. I told her she'd better keep her nose out of my business, and she said she didn't know what I was talking about. I really let her have it then."

"Let her have it?" Rhodes said.

"I called her a meddlesome bitch," Vernell said apologetically. "I was a little excited. I don't usually say things like that."

"What did she do when you said it?"

"She told me to get out of her house." Vernell inhaled deeply and let the smoke out in a sigh. "I guess I don't much blame her."

"And did you get out when she asked you to?"

"Yes. Why? Did she say I didn't? I wouldn't put it past her to lie about me."

"She didn't say anything," Rhodes said truthfully. "I don't suppose you got carried away with more than words, did you?"

"What do you mean by that?"

"You didn't hit her?"

"Hit her? Did she say that?" Vernell crushed the cigarette out savagely in the ashtray's panhandle region. "She is a bitch, then. I was feeling bad about saying that, but not anymore. I didn't lay a finger on her."

"Somebody did," Rhodes said.

"Maybe so, but it wasn't me, and she'd better not say so. If she does, I'll...well, I don't know what I'll do, but I'll do something."

"You won't have to," Rhodes said. "Somebody already has."

"Who?"

"That's what I'm trying to find out," Rhodes told her. "Right now, it looks like it was you."

Vernell looked worried. "I don't think I'm following you, Sheriff."

"It's like this," Rhodes said. "Yesterday afternoon, you went over to Faye's house. Is that right?"

"Yes, that's right."

"And the two of you had a pretty loud argument."

"Yes. It was loud."

"And then somebody killed Faye."

Vernell opened her mouth as if she were going to say something. But nothing came out, and after a second or two, she closed her mouth again.

"Someone hit Faye in the head," Rhodes said. "She fell down and didn't get up. Are you sure you didn't hit her?"

"I didn't!" Vernell said. "She was just fine when I left! I swear it!"

"As far as I've been able to find out, no one else was at Faye's house after you left. That doesn't look too good for you."

Vernell stood up and started pacing around the den. She came to a sheet of paper and kicked it out of her way. It fluttered up, then fell back to the floor. Vernell turned to face Rhodes.

"I didn't lay a hand on that woman," she said. "I don't know who told you I was there, but—"

Rhodes put up a hand. "Don't start that. I don't want you paying a visit to anybody else."

Vernell drew herself up straight, and when he saw the look in her blue eyes, Rhodes was glad there wasn't a cut-glass vase anywhere in the room.

"That's insulting," she said. "You're implying that I killed Faye because she told you about me and Ty. I can't believe you'd say something like that."

"I didn't mean to imply anything," Rhodes said. "I just don't want you to get in any more trouble than you already are."

"Why am I in trouble? I didn't do anything except have a little disagreement with someone."

"And it's just your bad luck that the someone's been murdered," Rhodes said. "I know. But I think it would be better if you didn't go looking for more trouble."

"Are you saying I'm under arrest?"

"No. I'm still investigating. I'm not ready to make any arrests."

"It's a good thing. You didn't even read me my rights."

People watched too much television, Rhodes thought, wondering if Vernell had learned about the Miranda warning on *Murder, She Wrote.*

"You can get back to work on your book," he said. "I might have some more questions for you later."

"I don't see how you can expect me to work after you've done this to me," Vernell said.

People always wanted to blame someone else, Rhodes thought. Never themselves. But he didn't really mind. He was used to it. Besides, as far as he could tell, no one had done anything to Vernell. Faye was a different story.

"If you can think of anything that might help me, give me a call," Rhodes said.

"Ha," said Vernell.

TWENTY-SEVEN

WHEN RHODES WALKED INTO the jail, Hack and Lawton looked up from where they were watching the last few minutes of *All My Children* on Hack's little TV set. Rhodes was convinced that the two of them had become addicted to the show, though they both denied it when he accused them. Nevertheless, he occasionally overheard them talking about the trials and tribulations of Erica Kane, among others on the show.

Hack saw that Rhodes was looking at them and snapped off the set.

"You got real trouble now," he said.

"You mean I didn't before?" Rhodes said.

"You just had the commissioners after you when Ty Berry got killed," Hack told him. "Now you got something worse."

"A lot worse," Lawton said from the other side of the room. "Ain't that right, Deputy?"

Buddy Reynolds, who'd been sitting at his desk and not watching the soap opera, nodded.

"Bad as it gets," he said.

They were at it again, Rhodes thought, and this time they even had Buddy helping them out.

"*Et tu,* Buddy?" Rhodes said.

"I recognize that," Hack said. "It's Latin, and it's from one of those Shakespeare plays. Bet I can tell you which one, too."

"Bet you can't," Lawton said.

"Julius Caesar," Hack said. "Ain't that right, Sheriff?"

"That's right, but it doesn't have a lot to do with what you're trying to tell me. At least I think you're trying to tell me something. Aren't you?"

"I already did. You're in big trouble now."

Rhodes tried not to sigh. He had two unsolved murders to deal with, and all he got was a hard time. And his eyes were itching.

"What kind of trouble?" he asked.

"You got the Chickenfooters against you," Hack said.

Rhodes looked at Buddy. "Tell me what he's talking about."

Buddy grinned. "He's trying to tell you that all Miz Knape's friends in that Chickenfoot group are ready to throw you out of office. Their good friend's been killed, and they think it's all your fault."

"They won't be votin' for you again," Hack said. "Not unless you put somebody in jail."

"And do it quick," Lawton added.

"I'd like to," Rhodes said. "But it's a little more complicated than they think. Maybe they can help me out, though. Buddy, did you get anything useful out of them?"

"Nope. They called Miz Knape's house twice, once about eight o'clock and again around eight-thirty. Didn't get an answer either time. They figured she'd just gone somewhere else and forgotten about the game, but when Miz Tabor called back this morning and didn't get anybody, she thought she'd better get in touch with us."

"Good thing they did," Hack said. "'Cept they should've done it last night."

"Too late to cry about that now," Buddy said. "Anyway, Miz Tabor's in that Historical Society of Faye's, and she's all upset about that part of it, too. The group was having a hard time holding together, since some of them wanted to support Ty Berry in that cemetery business, and without the president, the whole group might fall apart.''

That reminded Rhodes of something Ballinger had mentioned.

''The presidents of both those societies are dead now,'' he told Buddy. ''I want you to get a list of the members and see if you can come up with anything.''

''What should I look for?'' Buddy asked.

Rhodes didn't know what to tell him.

''You'll know it when you see it,'' he said. ''I hope.''

''Where'll I get the lists?''

Rhodes had an answer for that one.

''Faye and Ty both kept membership lists on their computers. I saw them, but I didn't read over them. You can go to their houses and print them out.''

''I don't know a printer from a sidesaddle,'' Buddy said.

''Take Hack with you, then. He can do it in ten seconds.''

''What about the phones?'' Hack wanted to know. ''Who's gonna take care of the calls if I leave?''

''Lawton,'' Rhodes said.

''Humpf,'' Hack said, as if to imply that Lawton knew about as much about telephones as Buddy knew about computers.

''I can handle it,'' Lawton said. ''I'll prob'ly treat people better than Hack does, too.''

''Humpf,'' Hack said again.

''Go on and get it done,'' Rhodes said.

''Where'll you be?'' Lawton asked.

''Ty Berry's funeral,'' Rhodes said.

HACK AND BUDDY LEFT, and Rhodes was almost out the
door when the phone rang. He stopped and waited to see
who was calling. It was Carl Mason, the sheriff of an
adjoining county, and he wanted to speak to Rhodes.

"We caught up with one of your fugitives," Mason
told Rhodes.

"I didn't know there was more than one," Rhodes
said.

"Well, then, that's the one we got. Name of Burt
Trask. Says he's never been in Blacklin County, never
been arrested for any reason, and he's the sole support
of his widowed mother and her poor, sickly old sister."

Rhodes had almost forgotten Trask, thanks to all the
other things that had happened.

"Sounds like a fine fella," Rhodes said. "Is any of
that the truth?"

"I wouldn't think so," Everett said. "He's been in and
out of the jail here so many times he's got his own mono-
grammed jump suit. His mother's got three boyfriends
that I know of, and they all take better care of her than
Trask does. Her poor, sickly old sister is maybe fifty and
healthy as a horse. Been a cook at the Dairy Queen for
as long as I can remember."

"Sounds like you know Burt's family pretty well."

"Yeah, since they always stick up for him. What'd you
get him for?"

"Drugs," Rhodes said.

There was a silence at the other end of the line. Finally
Mason said, "That's a new one. Burt's a guy who likes
to play around on the fringes, but we never got him for
anything like that before."

"I'd like to hear his story," Rhodes said. "I'll send
somebody to pick him up."

"I'll be waiting," Mason said.

RHODES HAD MISSED LUNCH, but he didn't have time to eat. He wouldn't even get any Vienna sausage today. But he couldn't let that bother him. He wanted to go to Berry's funeral just on the chance that he might learn something.

Unfortunately, he'd missed not only a chance at lunch but the first part of the services, which were held at the church. By the time he got there, people were already getting into their cars to go to the cemetery for the graveside service. Ruth Grady was there to lead the funeral procession and take care of the traffic, such as it was. Rhodes parked in the street and brought up the rear.

When he drove through the gates of the Clearview Cemetery, he thought about the ghost. As far as he knew, there hadn't been any sightings the previous night, and the jail had been quiet, too. Maybe he wouldn't be hearing any more about supernatural appearances. That would be fine with him. He was having enough trouble just dealing with natural problems.

Berry, as was fitting for someone who was president of the Sons and Daughters of Texas, was being buried in the oldest part of the cemetery, the one with graves dating back to the nineteenth century. There were still a few spots available there, but they were mostly all part of family plots and didn't come up for sale very often. Berry had likely paid for one some years ago.

The cars in the procession all parked along the side of the narrow road, with Rhodes bringing up the rear. He got out of his car and looked at the scene, which in a way reminded him of the one two days previously. There was the same fake grass, the same canvas canopy, the same folding chairs. There was the mound of earth and an open grave. But today there was sunshine instead of clouds, darkness, and rain. Berry would be going into the right grave this time, if there was such a thing as the right grave.

In the crowd were several people Rhodes had questioned about Berry's death. Vernell Lindsey was there, wearing a black dress. Rhodes couldn't see her feet from where he was standing, but he assumed she had on black shoes as well. Or maybe not.

Rhodes recognized several members of the Sons and Daughters of Texas, and a couple of the commissioners were there, Jay Bowman and Jerry Purcell. Rhodes spoke to them politely, and both of them asked him pointedly about the investigation. He told them that things were moving right along.

"And what about Faye Knape?" Purcell asked. "This kind of thing is bad for the county, Sheriff."

It was bad for Faye Knape, too, Rhodes thought. He said, "I'm sure I'll find out who did it. It just takes a little time."

"Well, time's one thing you don't have much of. We need some results."

"You'll get them," Rhodes said, hoping he sounded more confident than he felt.

Rhodes wasn't surprised to see the commissioners at the funeral, but he was a little surprised to see Melva Keeler, who was wearing a black dress, though she didn't look as good in it as Vernell did in hers.

Rhodes wondered what Melva was doing there. Maybe she was just one of those people who liked to go to funerals. There were plenty of people like that in Clearview. It didn't much matter to them who had died; they attended funerals like other people might go to a movie or to a good restaurant.

Melva hadn't mentioned knowing Ty Berry or being a member of the Sons and Daughters. But then Rhodes hadn't thought to ask her. He'd have to remember to do something about that later. He'd told Buddy not to bother questioning her, and that might have been a mistake. Rhodes thought that he had been making too many mistakes lately.

He tried to see what she was wearing on her feet, but there were too many people between them. Rhodes was pretty sure you couldn't get black fuzzy slippers, anyway.

Richard Rascoe was at the funeral, too. He came up to Rhodes and said, "I talked to Mr. Berry's cousin earlier today and told her I'd ordered her an angel like the one you saw in my store. No charge. She's going to have it put on Mr. Berry's monument."

Rhodes thought that was a nice gesture, but he wondered if it didn't mean that Rascoe had known Berry better than he'd let on.

"Did you and Berry have any other dealings?" Rhodes asked.

"Oh, no. But he was so interested when he came in the store that we had a long talk. I was sorry to hear he'd been killed. It's just a terrible thing. I hope you catch whoever did it. It's not a good feeling to know things like that can happen in small communities like this."

"I'm working on it," Rhodes said.

Rascoe drifted off after that, and Rhodes walked over near the canopy while the minister read a psalm and some verses from the New Testament. Then there was a prayer, and it was all over. Rhodes offered his condolences to Berry's cousin, Cathy Miller, who had sat dry-eyed through the service.

As soon as she turned away to speak to someone else, it occurred to Rhodes that he'd been lax again. He hadn't considered the fact that Cathy Miller was probably Ty Berry's sole heir. And Ty, who some years ago had retired early from some big chemical plant in south Texas before moving back to his hometown of Clearview, might have had a fairly sizable estate. That was one more thing for Rhodes to check into.

He walked over to say a word to Clyde Ballinger, who was hovering near the front of the canopy in case Ms. Miller needed his assistance. On his way over, Rhodes stooped down and picked up a couple of dark feathers and stuck them into one of the flower arrangements that had been placed nearby. Probably the wrong arrangement, but Rhodes wasn't too worried about it.

"Any word from Dr. White?" Rhodes asked Ballinger.

The funeral director shook his head. "Not yet. He'll get to Faye this evening, but it's pretty obvious how she died. I don't think he's going to come up with any surprises." Ballinger paused, then said, "It's a terrible thing, losing two fine citizens like that so close together. Who's going to take their place?"

Rhodes said he didn't know.

"Me neither. Sometimes I wonder what's going to happen to Clearview. It's not like it used to be."

Rhodes had been thinking the same thing a lot lately, but he didn't feel like telling Ballinger that. He just shrugged.

"Things change," he said.

"Never for the better, though," Ballinger said.

"Maybe it just seems that way to us old guys," Rhodes told him.

"What old guys?" Ballinger said, looking around. "I don't see any old guys here."

"Don't I wish," Rhodes said.

TWENTY-EIGHT

RHODES DIDN'T WAIT AROUND for the lowering of the casket. It was past time for his visit with the Packers, and he wanted to get on the road. He told Ruth to follow him. He wanted backup, since you could never be sure what might be waiting for you when you went to the Packers' place.

The Packers all lived out a mile or so from the tiny town of Obert on down the road from a man named Nard King, whom Rhodes had dealt with on another case, one that had involved, among other things, a couple of stolen emus.

Not so long ago, emus, and even fertile emu eggs, had been selling for astronomical prices. There were people who believed they were going to get rich raising and selling emus, and King was one of them. He'd moved to Blacklin County and built a new house alongside his new emu pens.

But he hadn't gotten rich. Rhodes wasn't sure that any of the emu farmers had. Emus turned out to be expensive to raise, and people like King, who'd thought emu steaks would soon be in high demand in restaurants all over the country, were amazed when the demand didn't develop. Nor did the demand for the myriad other products that supposedly could be produced from emus. The promised emu boom never happened, and King's new house was already looking old. His emu pens were empty. In a way, Rhodes felt sorry for the man, but when he remembered the circumstances of their meeting, he figured that King had probably gotten just about what he deserved.

There was no pickup parked in King's garage, and the whole place had a deserted and neglected look about it. Rhodes wondered if King had simply abandoned the place, packed up, and left the country.

He followed the road on down for another quarter of a mile to where it joined another county road that branched off to the right. The two roads made a sort of irregularly shaped Y, and in the crotch of the Y lived the Packers.

Rhodes drove in between the two cedar trees that stood at either side of the ruts leading into the yard. Ruth Grady followed close behind him.

At the back of the lot, fenced with drooping barbed wire, was their house. The roof sagged, the brick walls were cracked, and one side of the garage had collapsed inward. The house had been built forty years earlier and left vacant for twenty years before the Packers had moved in.

But after a year or so there hadn't been room for all of them in the house, and their dwellings had multiplied. To one side of the house there was a Winnebago that was never going to travel again. The tires had rotted off the wheels, which were sunk several inches into the ground. Most of the paint had long since disappeared, and the motor home seemed to be held together mainly by rust. The hood was up, but there was no engine inside the compartment. Both headlights were missing.

In front of the house was a double-wide mobile home in about the same condition as the Winnebago. The only difference was that the motor home was bigger and that it sat at a strange angle owing to the fact that concrete blocks had been slipped under one side of it before someone got too lazy to do the other side, the wheels of which, like those on the Winnebago, were sunk into the muddy yard.

An old Ford Thunderbird and two pickups sat in the yard. The pickups even looked as if they might run, but the Thunderbird wasn't going anywhere. It was up on blocks, and Rhodes could see two tires in the back seat. There was nothing resembling the Dodge Ram Rhodes had seen at the cemetery.

The whole place was so overgrown with trees, bushes, and vines that in the summertime it almost disappeared from sight. You could drive right by it and not even know there were people living within fifteen yards of the road.

Rhodes got out of the county car, and Ruth Grady joined him. There was no one to be seen, but he knew they were there, watching him from the house, the motor home, and the double-wide.

There was no grass in the yard, and a bunch of runty white leghorns with dirty feathers pecked listlessly at the mud while a rooster strutted around watching them. There was a sour smell, as if the septic tank were overdue for emptying, or maybe there wasn't a septic tank at all. Rhodes didn't think he wanted to know.

"Ah, the greater metropolitan area," Ruth said. "Sort of makes you want to move to the suburbs."

"Henry David Thoreau would be proud," Rhodes said.

He walked around the double-wide and went up to the house. There was a screen door hanging by one hinge. Rhodes moved it aside and knocked on the rotting facing.

The door opened and Rhodes found himself looking down at a boy of about five. His hair was slicked down, and he was so clean that he practically shone in the dim interior of the house. He had on a pair of jeans and a T-shirt that looked as if it had just come out of the dryer.

"Hi," he said.

"Hi," Rhodes said. "Anyone else at home?"

"My mama's here."

"Would you tell her I'd like to see her?"

"Sure."

The boy disappeared into the interior of the house.

"Wow," Ruth said.

"Don't be too impressed," Rhodes said. "The boy's a sure tip-off that they knew we were coming. They're not taking any chances on us calling Child Protective Services."

After a few seconds a woman came down the hall. She wasn't as spiffy as the boy, but she wasn't bad. And she wasn't the woman who'd been at the cemetery. Rhodes was sure of that. She was too tall and too thin.

"Hey, Sheriff," she said. "What can I do for you?"

Rhodes recognized her. She was Marlee, one of the daughters of old Abner Packer, who'd died a couple of years ago.

"I'd like to talk to Ferrell," Rhodes said.

Ferrell was Marlee's brother, the eldest of Abner's sons.

"He ain't around. Nobody here but me and Annie and the kids."

The boy who had answered the door came up quietly behind her and stood there looking up at Rhodes.

"Tobe's not here?" Rhodes said. "Roger? Dude?"

Those were the names of some of the Packer boys that he'd dealt with in the past. There were others he didn't know.

"All gone," Marlee said.

Rhodes wasn't really surprised. They must have left the county, hoping he'd give up on them. But if that was what they hoped, they didn't know him very well.

He was about to tell Marlee to give him a call when they got back when the boy said, "They're in school."

"School?" Rhodes said.

"You hush, Chris," Marlee said, pushing the boy farther behind her.

"What school?" Rhodes asked.

"He doesn't know what he's talking about," Marlee said.

"Do so," Chris said.

"No, you don't," Marlee said. "There's no school around here for people like us."

She turned around and pushed the boy down the hall, leaving the door open. Rhodes and Ruth waited for several minutes, but she didn't come back.

"What was that all about?" Ruth asked after a while.

"I'm not sure," Rhodes said. "But I do have an idea. Let's go."

They turned to leave, but Ruth tugged at Rhodes's sleeve.

"Look," she said, pointing.

There were freshly cut ruts in the mud beside the house, and the ruts led off into the trees in the back.

"Now, where do you suppose that track leads?" Ruth asked.

"I don't know," Rhodes said. "But I have an idea about that, too."

"So do I," Ruth said. "And I'll bet it's the same one."

"Then we'd better find out," Rhodes said.

They followed the ruts into the trees and out of them again into a field grown up in weeds. Another mobile home shell rusted in the field. The ruts cut through the weeds, up a hill, and straight through the barbed-wire fence. The fence hadn't been cut. Someone had just driven right over it, pulling down the old cedar posts and crushing the barbed wire into the mud.

The ruts ran downhill from the fence, into more trees.

"Isn't there a creek running along down there in those trees?" Ruth asked.

"Sandy Creek," Rhodes said. "There's a deep hole along in here somewhere that people used to come out and seine in the summer. That was a long time ago."

"I'd like to see that hole," Ruth said. "How deep would you say it is? Deep enough to cover a pickup truck?"

"It used to be. I'd guess it's silted up a lot over the years."

They walked down the hill and into the trees. It wasn't far from the first of the trees to the creek bank, where the ruts turned off to the right.

"That hole must be in that direction," Ruth said.

"I think that's right," Rhodes said.

They walked for about fifty yards. There was hardly any wind, and the trees were quiet. A little sunlight filtered through the leaves and speckled the muddy water. A turtle plopped off the bank with a splash. Suddenly the creek widened out.

"That's the place," Rhodes said.

"And it's not as deep as somebody thought it was," Ruth said. "Look."

Rhodes looked. The ruts turned and went down the bank and into the creek. About ten inches of the top of a Dodge Ram pickup cab stuck out of the water.

"They're no Ecksteins," Rhodes said.

"What?"

"Never mind. Looks like we both guessed right."

"Looks like it," Ruth said. "Now we know for sure who was shooting at us. So what do we do about it?"

"Go to school," Rhodes said.

TWENTY-NINE

WHEN HE GOT BACK to the county car, rhodes called Hack on the radio and told him to send Buddy Reynolds to pick up Burt Trask.

Rhodes hoped that if they picked up Trask, he'd think they knew more than they did about where he'd gotten the drugs. If he thought that, he might try to cut a deal by confirming Rhodes's suspicions about the source.

"How much do we know about Trask?" Hack asked.

Rhodes didn't want to give anything away, not on the radio. So he just said, "Enough."

"Speaking of knowing," Hack said, "since you didn't ask, I guess you don't want to hear what me and Buddy found out. I'll just send him on his way."

"Hold on," Rhodes said. "Of course I want to know what you found out. I thought it might take you longer to analyze the information."

"It's just a bunch of names. How long could it take?"

"What I meant was I didn't think Buddy would come up with anything this soon."

"How do you know it was Buddy that came up with it? It could've been me."

Rhodes got a tight grip on his patience and said, "Was it you?"

"Well, no, it wasn't. It was Buddy. But it could've been me."

"You're right. I'm surprised it wasn't, considering how smart you are. Now, are you going to tell me what it was, or are you going to make me come back to the jail?"

"I think you better come back here," Hack said. "You wouldn't want this goin' out over the air."

"Ruth and I have to go somewhere else," Rhodes said. "I'll get back there as soon as I can."

"Where you gonna be?" Hack asked.

"I wouldn't want that going out over the air," Rhodes said.

THE WAY RHODES FIGURED IT, there was only one kind of school the Packers would be interested in attending, and that was the kind that might be run by a couple of guys like Rapper and Nellie. Rhodes had heard of a number of cases where people with the know-how were more than willing to teach others to use the Nazi cook method of making methamphetamine, but the tuition would be high. According to what Rhodes had read, it could run as high as ten thousand dollars a person, though Rapper might be willing to give group discounts to people like the Packers.

And of course the Packers, never having done an honest day's work in their lives, would be ideal candidates for enrollment in a class on drug making. The only problem they'd have would be coming up with the tuition. As far as Rhodes knew, there weren't any financial aid programs for courses in cooking up drugs. The Packers were, however, nothing if not resourceful. They'd figure out a way to get the money for the class, even if it meant stealing from cemeteries.

Burt Trask might be interested in attending class, too, but a guy like Burt would want to try the merchandise first. For all Rhodes knew, the Packers had tried it, too. Rapper wouldn't mind giving out a free sample, not as long as he thought he had a prospective student on the hook.

Rhodes knew things might not work out to be exactly the way he had them figured, but it all seemed right to him. Drugs, Rapper, the Packers: it all fit.

And the idea of the classes fit, too. Rapper would be wary of selling drugs, considering his previous experiences, but he wouldn't be doing the actual selling. He'd just be making them, in his newly created role of Professor of Kitchen Chemistry. He'd think that teaching others to make the drugs and then letting them take the risks of selling the final product would be a lot safer than selling them himself.

Naturally he'd think he could get away with it in Blacklin County. After all, he'd gotten away with just about everything else he'd tried there, if you didn't count little things like a couple of missing fingers and a permanent limp.

Rhodes explained all that to Ruth, who agreed it made sense.

"And you think they're out there at that house near Milsby, cooking up a batch right now?" she said.

"I'd say it's a good possibility."

"You want to go see if you're right?"

"I can't think of a better way to find out," Rhodes said.

"Then let's go."

"We'll take the shortcut," Rhodes said.

THERE WERE TWO WAYS to get from Obert to Milsby. One of them was to go back to Clearview first, traveling only the highways. That was the easy way.

The shortcut, on the other hand, meant traveling on graveled county roads. It had the advantage of being considerably more scenic, and it didn't take quite as long, unless you got behind someone driving a tractor or harvester, in which case it could take a lot longer. Rhodes thought it was worth taking a chance.

The road led by the old college that had long ago fallen into near-ruin. Several people had tried unsuccessfully to restore it, and recently a man named Wendell Anders had finally finished the job. The sun shone on the worn stone walls, and Rhodes wondered what Anders had planned for the building.

Rhodes remembered that the building was where he had encountered what someone had reported to him as a ghost. It hadn't been a ghost, of course, but the memory made Rhodes think about the latest ghostly sightings. He didn't believe in ghosts, but he believed in what he could see himself. And he'd certainly seen *something* in the Clearview Cemetery. So had those teenagers.

But what had they seen? Rhodes didn't have an answer for that one. Not yet. Something was itching at the back of his mind, and he could almost make the connections. But not quite. He'd have to keep worrying at it.

WHEN RHODES ARRIVED about a quarter of a mile from the house that Rapper was leasing, he was a little disappointed. He could see no cars or trucks parked anywhere around the house. If Rapper had any pupils, they were keeping their transportation out of sight. For a second Rhodes entertained the idea of Rapper driving a big yellow school bus around the county to pick everyone up, making sure they all had their lunches in little brown bags and that everyone got to class on time.

Rhodes pulled the car over to the side of the road and stopped. Ruth stopped behind him, and they got out.

"What do you think?" Ruth asked.

"I don't see any cars," Rhodes said.

"There's a little stand of trees on down the road," Ruth said. "They could be parked in there. If they drove them in far enough, they'd be hidden from the road. They'd have to walk a little way, but they wouldn't mind that."

"We could check," Rhodes said. "If we do that, though, they'll see us when we drive by."

Ruth shrugged. "No use in giving them a warning like that. Let's just drive up in the yard and say hello."

Rhodes thought it over and came up with what he thought was a better idea.

"I'll tell you what," he said. "You go down to the trees and see if the cars are there. If they are, stay there and watch them. I'll try the house."

"All right," Ruth said. "But be careful. You never can tell what someone like Rapper might do."

"I know," Rhodes said. "That's what makes this job so much fun."

THE WORD *FUN* gave Rhodes another idea that he decided was worth a try. After Ruth swung her car around his and headed for the trees, he let her get a good head start. Then he turned on his light bar and siren and floored the accelerator, throwing gravel and mud against the car's undercarriage and sending it spewing out behind him. The car rocked and bounced along the road. When Rhodes wrenched it into the turn into Rapper's yard, the tires lost all traction. The car slewed around a hundred and eighty degrees, slopping a wave of mud two or three feet high across the yard.

The flamboyant entrance had the effect Rhodes hoped for. He didn't have a warrant, and he was sure Rapper would never have let him inside the house. If everyone had kept quiet, Rhodes might never have been sure what was going on in there.

But surprise and panic were wonderful partners when they were combined with a house full of guilty consciences. By the time Rhodes had gotten out of the car and drawn his pistol, people were jumping out of windows and doors and running for their lives.

Rhodes fired a shot into the air.

"Everybody freeze!" he yelled.

No one paid any attention, but Rhodes hadn't really expected them to. He wasn't too worried that they'd get away. Ruth was at the cars, or she was if they'd guessed correctly, so no one would be going anywhere.

Except for Rapper and Nellie. Rhodes had forgotten about the motorcycles, and, sure enough, he heard them fire up inside the chicken house, the noise of their engines reverberating off the tin walls like thunder.

The two bikers came roaring out of the chicken house while everyone else scattered across the field. Rhodes had nearly been run down by Rapper more than once, so he got behind his car, where Rapper would find it almost impossible to run over him.

Rapper didn't even try. He and Nellie zoomed past the car, mud flying away from the spinning wheels of their bikes. They took off down the road without so much as a backward glance at Rhodes.

Rhodes watched them go. He could catch up with them later. Right now he wanted to deal with the people who were running across the field toward the trees. He'd recognized several of them, including Ferrell and Dude Packer.

But one of them was someone he hadn't been expecting: Nard King. Obviously the emu business was even worse than Rhodes had thought. And Nard was willing to take a little trip over to the shady side in order to make a financial recovery. When he thought about his previous dealings with Nard, Rhodes wasn't at all surprised.

But Nard wasn't the same kind of criminal that the Packers were. Rhodes thought he might be the weak link, so he started after him on foot. Rhodes thought he could catch up with King, and there was no use taking a chance of getting the county car stuck in a muddy field.

He'd gotten about halfway across the yard when the house exploded.

Rhodes almost had time to think that Rapper had outsmarted him again, but everything happened too fast for that. Rhodes barely glimpsed the orange fireball that lifted the roof and bulged the walls of the house outward. Then the force of the blast picked him up and threw him away.

THIRTY

THE NEXT THING Rhodes knew, he was lying flat on his back in the mud, looking up at the blue sky. A buzzard was making wide, lazy circles, high and faraway.

There was a railroad track running right through the middle of Rhodes's head, and the afternoon freight was rumbling along the steel rails and clicking over the cross-ties, right on time.

Except that it had been years since there'd been an afternoon freight in Blacklin County, and even if there had been, the tracks wouldn't have been in Rhodes's head.

Rhodes sat up and looked around. There were a few shards of glass sticking out of the mud, and Rhodes knew he was lucky that one of them hadn't hit some vital part of his anatomy. A few loose boards and some shingles lay nearby.

The house that Rapper and his pals had so recently deserted was blazing, and Rhodes felt the heat burn his face. He struggled to his feet and moved farther away. He thought about calling the Clearview Volunteer Fire Department, but the house was nothing but old, dry wood, and Rhodes knew that there would be nothing left of it but smoldering ash by the time he reached his car radio.

He knew, too, that the flames should be making a crackling sound and that he should be able to hear the popping of the burning wood, but all he could hear was a steady roar.

Or maybe that wasn't it. Maybe he was simply hearing nothing at all. He wondered what kind of explosive Rapper had used, not that it mattered. Whatever it had been, it had been very effective, and it had undoubtedly destroyed everything in the old house, including any signs of drug manufacture. So Rapper wouldn't be arrested for drugs, and unless there was some way to prove what he'd done to the house, he'd get away with that, too.

And there wasn't going to be any way to prove what he'd done. There wasn't going to be enough left to give even the best arson investigator a clue, and Blacklin County didn't have an arson investigator of any kind if you didn't count Rhodes.

Rhodes saw Ruth Grady drive into the yard. She got out of the car and ran toward him. He could see her mouth moving, but he couldn't hear what she was saying. He pointed to his ear and shook his head.

When she got closer, she mouthed some words very slowly. It appeared to Rhodes that she was saying, "Are you all right?"

He hoped so. He didn't think the hearing loss would last long, and he didn't seem to have any other terrible aches and pains beyond what seemed to be some minor muscle strains in his back and shoulders. He twisted his body to the left and right to see if everything was working. It was.

"What happened to the cars?" he asked.

He couldn't even hear his own voice. He knew he was saying the words, but they didn't seem to be coming out.

Ruth shrugged, which Rhodes took to mean that as soon as the house exploded, she'd left the cars and come back to see about him. That meant that everyone had gotten away. It didn't really matter. Both Ruth and Rhodes had seen the Packers and Nard King, and they could pick them up at any time, just as long as they stayed in the county.

Rhodes looked over Ruth's shoulder at the house, or what was left of it. It was burning like tinder.

Ruth took out a notepad, flipped it open, and wrote, "Can you drive?" on a blank page with a ballpoint pen.

Rhodes nodded, but he wasn't ready to go yet. He wanted to see if Rapper and Nellie had left anything in the chicken house. He told Ruth what he was going to do, and she followed him.

The old chicken house smelled of must and dust and mold and ancient chicken droppings, but there was nothing inside it. Rapper and Nellie traveled light, and any possessions they hadn't kept on the bikes were gone in the flames that had destroyed the house.

"Let's go back to town," Rhodes said.

BY THE TIME they got back to the jail, Rhodes's hearing was starting to return. It would probably be days before he could hear normally, but at least he should be able to get along.

When he went inside, Hack said something, but Rhodes didn't quite get it. Ruth went over to Hack and explained the situation.

"That's why he looks like he's been shot out of a cannon, then," Hack said.

He must have said it loudly, since Rhodes could make out nearly all the words. Rhodes was watching him, too, which helped.

"Ivy's not gonna like it that you've been takin' chances again," Hack said.

Rhodes didn't need Hack to tell him that. He'd have to get cleaned up before he saw Ivy, and when he told her about what had happened, he'd have to make it sound as if there had been no danger involved.

"Did ever'body get away?" Hack asked. "Rapper and all?"

Rhodes nodded.

"Figgers," Hack said. "Pretty smart of Rapper, though, blowin' up the house like that. You gotta admire a man who plans ahead."

Rhodes didn't see anything admirable about it.

"Prob'ly saw you comin', too," Hack said. "Soon's he did, he lit the fuse. Gotta hand it to him."

Rhodes thought about it. He'd been wrong when he believed his sudden appearance with his siren howling and light bar flashing had emptied the house. It hadn't been that at all. Rapper had spotted Ruth when she drove by, set up his explosion, and told everyone to clear out. It was every man for himself, as far as Rapper was concerned, and there would be no tuition refund at Rapper U.

Rhodes wished things had worked out differently, but he had to move on. So he asked Hack what he and Buddy had found out.

"Found out about what?" Hack asked. "We found out a couple of things."

Rhodes didn't really feel like waiting for Hack to get to the point in his usual roundabout way.

"Just tell me something," he said.

"I'll start with the cats, then," Hack said.

Rhodes had forgotten about the cats, and he wasn't so sure he wanted to know about them. But there was no stopping Hack now.

"Those cats of Miz Knape's were mighty lonesome," Hack said. "I guess she must've given them a lot of attention. They came out and rubbed up against our legs, purrin' so hard they were practically vibratin'. They need somebody to take care of them.''

He stopped talking and gave Rhodes a pointed look.

"I have two dogs," Rhodes said, as if that would let him off the hook.

"Don't matter," Hack said. "Cats and dogs can get along just fine if they want to, and these'd want to. You can't just leave 'em in that house all by themselves.''

"I'm allergic to cats," Rhodes said. "They make me sneeze, and they don't like me. They didn't purr when I was there. They hid from me.''

"They'd get used to you," Hack said.

"Not me. They just plain didn't like me, either that or they were scared of me.''

"Somebody's gotta take care of 'em," Hack said.

Rhodes looked at Ruth.

"Don't look at me," she said. "I love cats, but they make me break out in a rash.''

Then she blushed. Rhodes didn't think he'd ever seen her blush before.

"Boyfriend," Hack said.

Ruth turned to him and said something that Rhodes couldn't hear. Then she turned back.

"Hack's right. I've been going with somebody, and he doesn't like cats at all.''

Rhodes could understand why some people didn't like cats, even though he was fond of them himself. In fact, he liked them a lot. He just couldn't stand being around them.

"Those cats'd like you if you gave 'em a chance," Hack told Rhodes. "They need somebody.''

"I can't take those cats," Rhodes said. "It's impossible.''

"Dr. White could give you something for that allergy," Hack said.

"No," Rhodes said. "I don't like taking things that I don't really need."

"You'd need it if you had the cats," Hack said.

"Forget it," Rhodes told him.

"If you say so. Those cats're sure in pitiful shape with Miz Knape dead and gone, though."

"What about her family?" Rhodes asked, feeling desperate. "Hadn't thought about that," Hack said. "She has a son and a daughter. Somebody's gonna have to call them."

"I can't talk on the phone," Rhodes said, pointing to his ear. "Call Clyde Ballinger and let him do it. I'm sure one of them will want the cats."

"Maybe," Hack said. "Maybe not."

Rhodes chose not to think about the "maybe not" possibility. There was no way he was taking the cats.

"What about the members of those historical societies?" he asked. "You said you found out something important about them."

"You can prob'ly figger it out for yourself," Hack said, and he handed Rhodes two sheets of paper.

Rhodes looked them over. One was headed "Sons and Daughters of Texas Membership Roll." The other said that it contained the names of "Members in Good Standing, Clearview Historical Society."

Rhodes read down both lists, then handed the papers back to Hack.

"Interestin' stuff, huh?" Hack said. "You see what it is we found out?"

Rhodes nodded. Everyone knew that the two associations were rivals and that their rivalry was heated. Rhodes wouldn't have thought that anyone would want to belong to both groups.

But someone did.

Melva Keeler.

THIRTY-ONE

RHODES KNEW IT WAS TIME to talk to Melva Keeler again, but he also wanted Ruth to check up on Cathy Miller's whereabouts on the night Berry had died. She would have had plenty of time to kill him and drive back to Austin before anyone even knew he was dead.

"Do you really think she killed him?" Ruth asked when Rhodes told her what he wanted her to do.

Rhodes heard her, though not very well, and now he could also hear a painful ringing in his head. It no longer sounded like a train.

"I don't know," Rhodes said. "It's something we have to check on."

"What about those Packers?" Hack asked. "I'll bet they're the ones that killed him. He was out there waitin' for somebody to show up, and sure enough, somebody did. But he made the mistake of tryin' to deal with them himself instead of givin' us a call like he should have done. Bang. He's dead. Those Packers would just as soon kill a fella as look at him. Rather kill him, prob'ly. They're mean right down to the bone, those Packers."

"The Packers are mean, all right," Rhodes said, "but you wouldn't catch them using a .22. They'd just as soon use a peashooter. They're into nine-millimeter automatics and assault rifles. And if they'd been the ones to kill Berry, they wouldn't have left the cemetery empty-handed. They'd have taken what they came for."

"They might've been scared," Hack said.

"Maybe, but they would have torn the place up with

their truck. Whoever killed Ty was parked on the road and didn't leave tracks.''

"What about Rapper and that friend of his, Nellie? They're killers if there ever was a pair of 'em.''

"You're probably right,'' Rhodes said. "But why would they want to kill Ty?''

"You're the sheriff. You're supposed to figger it out.''

"That's what I'm trying to do,'' Rhodes said.

DRIVING TO Melva Keeler's house, Rhodes thought about everything that had happened and all that he knew or had guessed. It certainly seemed possible that Faye knew about Ty Berry's interest in the buildings that she owned and that she, and her husband before her, had so seriously neglected over the course of the years.

If Ty had threatened to reveal her ownership to the members of the Historical Society, Faye might well have felt desperate enough to kill him. And the pistol Rhodes had found in her desk could be the one that did the job. In fact, he suspected that it was, though proving it was a different matter and would likely be impossible.

Ty wouldn't have felt threatened by Faye, and if she had met him in the cemetery, she could easily have gotten close enough to shoot him. Rhodes would have been willing to bet that Faye hadn't been an expert with a pistol. Even if she had been, the derringer wouldn't have been accurate at a range of more than a few feet.

As much satisfaction as it would have given Rhodes to blame the Packers or Rapper for Ty's death, Faye was a much more likely suspect.

But Rhodes wondered about the pistol and where it could have come from. Faye's husband had owned guns, true, but she'd sold them and claimed to know nothing about how to use them. She must have been lying, at least in part. She could have sold all but one of her husband's guns and kept that one back for personal protection. Lots of single women, at least in Texas, kept a gun in the house.

The idea of keeping a pistol around for personal protection would explain why the pistol had been in her desk instead of in the gun cabinet, though Rhodes didn't really understand why the cabinet was still there. Why hadn't Faye gotten rid of it when she sold the guns?

And, even more to the point, who had killed Faye? Rhodes had originally thought Vernell Lindsey had the best motive. Faye had tried to shift suspicion onto her for Ty's death, after all, and Vernell hadn't been the least bit happy about that. She'd been seen arguing with Faye on the afternoon of her death, and she'd been alone inside the house with her. Things didn't look good for Vernell.

But they didn't look all that good for Melva Keeler, either. Why hadn't she mentioned that she was a member of the Historical Society when she'd talked to Rhodes earlier? And why hadn't she said anything about being a member of Berry's group?

Rhodes, of course, hadn't asked her, but it seemed pretty strange to him that she hadn't mentioned the coincidence of both presidents being murdered. Rhodes had to admit that it hadn't occurred to him, but it had to Clyde Ballinger, who wasn't affiliated with either group. Surely it must have occurred to Melva.

And maybe it had. Maybe she'd decided to unify the two groups by eliminating the leaders and taking over as president of both clubs. Or if Faye had killed Ty, maybe Melva had seen her opportunity and gotten Faye out of the way, planning to blame the murder on Vernell after she'd seen the two of them having their argument.

The more Rhodes thought about that possibility, the

better he liked it. It was too bad that cut-glass vases didn't take fingerprints. That would have made proving his theory a whole lot easier.

MELVA KEELER had changed out of her black dress into a pair of baggy black pants and a blue blouse with teddy bears on it. She was wearing the fuzzy slippers, and she didn't seem surprised to see Rhodes.

After Rhodes apologized for his appearance, she invited him in, and they sat in the living room to talk.

"I thought you'd be back," she told Rhodes.

"What made you think that?" Rhodes asked, looking around the room, interested to see that Melva had a bookcase full of paperbacks, all of which appeared to be romance novels.

"I knew you'd have some more questions for me," she said. "I've thought of several more things about Faye that you probably need to know."

Rhodes's hearing had improved. "For example?" he asked.

Melva shifted in her chair. "Yesterday wasn't the first time that she and Vernell Lindsey had a falling out."

Rhodes wondered whether this was just another attempt to shift suspicion or if it might mean something. He could always check it out with Vernell.

He said, "I take it that Mrs. Knape confided in you."

"Not often, but we were members of the Historical Society, you know."

"Yes, I do know. And I know that you're also a member of the Sons and Daughters of Texas. In fact, you're the only person in the county who's a member of both those groups."

Melva nodded. "That's right. I've always believed that

the best way to bring about peace and harmony between two opposing forces was to work from the inside.''

"So you were working to get the two groups to combine into one?''

"Oh, no. I knew there was no hope of that. Too many personality conflicts. I just wanted to see if there wasn't some way to get them to work together for the same goals. You remember what happened about that cabin?''

Rhodes remembered, all right. The cabin that Melva meant was a part of the county's history, and it had caused quite a bit of trouble between the Sons and Daughters and the members of the Historical Society. There had been a couple of murders connected with it, too, which is how Rhodes had met Berry in the first place.

"That's what I wanted to avoid,'' Melva said. "Things like that. It was all so unpleasant. I thought I could convince everyone that it would be better to work together on common projects. We could do so much more good for the county that way, you see.''

Rhodes saw.

"One way to do that,'' he said, "might be to kill the presidents and take over yourself. You could run the whole show.''

Melva sat up straight and opened her mouth to take a deep breath. She let it out slowly, and then she laughed.

"My word, Sheriff, you must be joking.''

"I wish I were. Even if you didn't kill Ty Berry, you could have killed Faye. You could have walked across the street and done it after Vernell Lindsey left.''

Melva sobered. "You can't really think I'd kill anybody, Sheriff. I'm the one who wants to work for peace and harmony. You can't have those things if you're running around and killing people.''

She sounded so sincere that Rhodes almost believed her.

"Do you have any guns in the house?" he asked.

"Oh, no. I don't like guns. They're the cause of so much trouble, you see. I think we can all work out our problems without resorting to shooting each other, don't you?"

"It would be nice if we could," Rhodes said, thinking about something he'd heard or read somewhere about a woman who protested too much.

"What about Faye?" he asked. "Did she keep a gun in the house?"

"My word. I wouldn't know about that, even if she did. I visited her now and then, not what you could call often, and I certainly never saw one. I know that her husband had guns, but she would never have said anything to me about having one for herself. She knew how I felt about them."

Rhodes could see he wasn't going to get any help on that subject.

He said, "You say you didn't see anyone else at Mrs. Knape's house yesterday after Vernell left?"

"No, I didn't, but that doesn't mean no one was there. She has, or *had,* I guess, a lot of trees in her yard. After dark, it's hard to tell if someone's parked in her driveway."

"But you didn't go over there."

"Certainly not. Believe me, Sheriff, I'd never kill anyone. Why, I hardly ever even get angry."

"That must be nice," Rhodes said.

"Well, it is. I like to say that nobody can get my goat, because I don't let them know where it's tied up." She laughed. "And speaking of goats, that's what Faye and Mrs. Lindsey had an argument about once before. You could ask the members of the society about it. We all heard the story."

"What story?" Rhodes asked.

"I suppose you know that Vernell has goats in her yard," Melva said.

Rhodes said that he knew.

"And that they get out all the time."

Rhodes admitted that he knew that, too.

"We get calls about that now and then," he said.

"And some of the callers don't tell you who they are, I'll bet. One of them was probably Faye. She thought it was wrong to keep goats in town. She said it spoiled the look of the whole community when the first thing you saw when you drove into town was a yard full of goats. She went to see Vernell and told her she ought to get rid of them. Vernell told her the goats were none of her damned business. I don't mean to cuss, Sheriff, but that's what Faye told us she said."

Vernell hadn't mentioned that little bit of information. Neither had Faye, for that matter. Rhodes could see why.

But that didn't let Melva off the hook.

"Did anyone come by to see Faye earlier, before Vernell?" he asked.

"Not that I know of. Faye was gone most of the day. You know how she is, Sheriff. Or was. She liked to be busy all the time."

Rhodes could see that he wasn't going to get anywhere with Melva Keeler. She wasn't going to break down and confess, and she was going to keep shifting suspicion to other people. But if she was guilty, sooner or later she would slip up. Or so Rhodes told himself. It happened that way sometimes.

Of course it could be that she wasn't shifting suspicion

at all and that Vernell Lindsey really did have something more to hide.

Which meant that he'd have to pay her another visit, though not until he'd gone home and cleaned up. He was afraid it was already too late to get himself in decent shape before Ivy got home, but he'd have to do the best he could.

He thanked Melva for her help, such as it had been, and left. There was a high bank of dark clouds in the north, which could mean that more rain was on the way.

Just what we need, Rhodes thought, and then he wondered about Faye Knape's cats. He didn't know how often cats had to be fed, but those three hadn't had any food set out since that morning. He thought he'd better go across the street and see about them.

The house was dark, and Rhodes turned on the light in the hall. There were no cats to be seen.

He walked down the hall, past the living room. He turned on the light in there and looked around. Things were exactly as he'd left them that morning. No cats.

He went on to the back porch and checked the food bowls. They weren't empty, but most of the food was gone. Rhodes decided it wouldn't hurt to put a little food out for the night, so he got the dry food out of the cabinet. This time when the food rattled into the bowls, all three cats came running. The big gray tabby was in the lead. The other two were solid black, with yellow eyes. They looked like a couple of extras in a movie about witches.

None of the three rushed up to Rhodes to brush against his legs. They didn't purr. But they didn't run away, either. They watched him cautiously, ready to run for cover at the slightest threatening move.

Rhodes didn't plan to threaten them, but he did think their water needed changing. He picked up two of the bowls to take them into the kitchen. The cats turned and fled.

Rhodes emptied the two bowls into the sink and refilled them, then did the same with the third bowl. When he set that one on the floor, all three cats were back, watching him. The big gray tabby was swishing its tail. The two black ones appeared to be considering whether to make a sneak attack on the food bowls or simply disappear.

"I'm not going to hurt anybody," Rhodes said, but when he started out of the room, the cats ran away again.

Outside the house, Rhodes took a deep breath. For some reason, his eyes didn't seem to be itching as much as he thought they would, and he didn't feel the urge to sneeze. He wasn't quite sure what that meant, but he knew one thing: it didn't mean that he was going to be adopting any cats.

He kept telling himself that all the way home.

THIRTY-TWO

"YOU LOOK LIKE you had fun today," Ivy said when Rhodes walked in. "I don't think Yancey recognizes you."

Yancey was bouncing around like a fur-coated rubber ball, yipping madly, and trying to sink his sharp little teeth into Rhodes's ankles.

"He does that all the time," Rhodes said. "That's his normal behavior. My looks don't have anything to do with it."

He went to the bathroom and cleaned himself up, then went into the bedroom and changed clothes. When he came out of the bedroom, Yancey attacked again.

"See what I mean?" Rhodes said.

"You could be right," Ivy said.

She shooed Yancey away. He stalked over to a chair and lay down under it, laying his chin on his front paws and watching them with a hurt look.

"Why don't you tell me how you made such a mess of yourself?" Ivy said.

Rhodes did. When he was finished, Ivy wasn't smiling, though he'd done his best to minimize any danger to himself.

"One night you're getting shot at in a cemetery," she said, "and the next day you're getting blown up in the country. You're going to have to promise me that you'll be more careful."

Rhodes promised. Both of them knew that he meant it. They both also knew that it wouldn't change a thing.

"Where would you like to eat tonight?" Rhodes asked.

Ivy said that she'd picked up some barbecue on the way home.

"I'll warm it up," she said. "After we eat, we can watch TV."

"That sounds good," Rhodes said. "Except that I have something else I need to do."

"What's that?"

"Bust some ghosts. Want to come along?"

"Am I allowed to ride with you when you're on official county business?"

"This isn't all that official," Rhodes said. "I'm pretty sure I know what's been happening in the Clearview Cemetery, though, and I'm going to check it out."

"Couldn't you do it in the daytime?"

"I have a couple of other things to do tomorrow."

"Like solving a murder," Ivy said. "I know. Will there be any shooting?"

"I hope not," Rhodes said.

"Good. Then I'll go with you. I've always wanted to see a ghost. We are going to see a ghost, aren't we?"

"Could be," Rhodes said.

THE BARBECUE was excellent, thinly sliced brisket with no detectable fat, just the way Rhodes liked it. And the sauce was sweet and spicy at the same time, so spicy that Rhodes didn't even need any jalapeños on the side.

Yancey sat by during the meal, watching them, still hurt that Ivy had fussed at him. But he was quiet, which Rhodes appreciated.

When they had finished eating, Rhodes helped Ivy clean the table and then took Yancey out in the back yard so that he and Speedo could race around and chase each other for a while. After they were tired of that, Rhodes tossed an old rubber hamburger for them to run after, argue over, and protect from Rhodes, who always managed to pry it from their jaws and give it another toss.

When Ivy came out, Yancey was pooped, and so was Rhodes, but Speedo seemed to have gotten his second wind. He was mouthing the hamburger and growling, trying to get Yancey interested, but Yancey just sat and watched him.

"Want to take Speedo with us?" Ivy asked.

"I don't think we'd want him running around loose in the cemetery," Rhodes said. "He might cause more damage than the ghosts. Besides, we're going in the county car, not the Edsel. This is more or less official."

"All right," Ivy said. "Come on, Yancey."

Yancey flounced across the yard, and Ivy let him inside the house.

"Looks like rain," she said when she came back.

"Maybe it'll hold off until we get through," Rhodes said.

THEY DROVE BY the jail first, and Hack had good news and bad news.

"Which one do you want first?" he asked.

Rhodes looked at Ivy, who smiled. Rhodes had told her about the game Hack and Lawton loved to play.

"Give me the bad news," Rhodes said.

"Right. Here it is. Clyde Ballinger called Faye's kids, who were naturally all shook up about what happened to her. They're talkin' about comin' down tomorrow and bringing half the reporters in Texas with 'em. They told Clyde that if a little old lady could be murdered in cold blood in a small Texas town, there must be something wrong with the law enforcement, and they'd go to the commissioners and ask for a full investigation."

"Great," Rhodes said. "The commissioners are upset enough as it is."

"Yeah," Hack said. "And that's not all."

"I know," Rhodes said. "There's the good news."

Hack shook his head. "Not yet. We got more bad news to go with the first."

"Tell me," Rhodes said.

"They don't want the cats," Hack said.

"Cats?" Ivy said. "What cats?"

Hack feigned surprise. "He didn't tell you about the cats?"

"No," Ivy said. She looked at Rhodes. "He didn't tell me about the cats."

Rhodes thought that the time to strangle Hack had finally arrived. But he couldn't do it, not with Ivy there as a witness. He put up his hands.

"I forgot," he said.

"Sure," Hack said. "It's easy to forget three poor kitties starved for affection, who'll prob'ly have to be put to sleep because nobody'll take 'em in."

"You'd think Faye's children would want them," Rhodes said defensively. "Something to remember their mother by."

"We could take them," Ivy said.

"No, we couldn't," Rhodes said. "I'm allergic. And the dogs would hate them."

"We'll talk about it," Ivy said, and Rhodes knew he was doomed.

"What's the good news?" he asked. "You did say there was some good news, didn't you?"

Hack grinned. "Sure thing. Buddy brought in that Trask fella, and he's singin' like Bing Crosby."

"What's the tune?" Rhodes asked.

"About what you thought," Hack said. "He started talkin' by the time Buddy got him in the car. He wants a deal. So Buddy gave him the Miranda and listened to what he had to say. Course Buddy didn't promise him anything, but the guy talked anyway."

"And he said?"

"He said he got the dope from Rapper. It was supposed to be a sample of the kind of thing Rapper was gonna teach him to cook up. He didn't try it himself, naturally. Never touches the stuff."

"Naturally," Rhodes said, glad to know he'd been right about Rapper. "What kind of deal did he want?"

"Says he'll testify against Rapper if we'll let him off on the possession charges."

"What about leaving the scene of an accident?"

"He didn't mention that."

Rhodes smiled. "Good. We can promise him a deal on the possession charge and then nail him on the other one."

"Are you sure he won't think of that?" Ivy asked.

"He may be singing like Crosby," Rhodes said. "But he's no Eckstine."

Ivy looked at him blankly.

"It's complicated," Rhodes said. "Someday I'll explain it."

"I'd probably be better off if you didn't."

"True. Well, now that we have that taken care of, let's go to the cemetery."

"What're you gonna do out there?" Hack wanted to know.

"Just call us the Ghost Breakers," Rhodes said.

"Busters," Hack said.

Rhodes shook his head. "Wrong movie. *The Ghost*

Breakers is more my speed. Bob Hope, Paulette Goddard."

Hack thought it over, then said, "Catchers, then. *Ghost Catchers* had Olsen and Johnson. I'd say that's even more your speed."

"You could be right," Rhodes told him.

"Amen," Ivy said.

THIRTY-THREE

THE WIND WAS kicking up by the time they got to the cemetery, and the clouds were getting thick. The night was very dark.

"Perfect night for ghosts," Ivy said. "You couldn't have planned it better."

"You should have been out here with me the other night," Rhodes said. "When it was thundering and lightning. And raining. That was better."

"I think we can do without the rain."

"Me, too. But I'd like to find those ghosts."

"You know something?" Ivy said. "You're just as bad as Hack in your own little way."

"What little way?"

"You still haven't told me what the ghost is or how you know about it."

"That's because I don't know. I just suspect."

"Whatever. You could still tell me."

"I guess you're right," Rhodes said. "The truth is, there's no such thing as ghosts."

"See what I mean? You're just like him. You've been around that jail too long."

"You might have a point," Rhodes admitted.

"So tell me."

Rhodes stopped the car. They were parked not far from where Ty Berry had been buried that afternoon. The canopy and chairs were gone, and the raw earth mounded over his grave was no longer covered by a carpet of fake green grass.

"Emus," Rhodes said.

"Emus?" Ivy didn't sound convinced. "How on earth did you get from ghosts to emus?"

"It's hard to explain."

"Try," Ivy said.

The trouble was that Rhodes couldn't really explain it, not even to himself. He worked mostly by intuition and hunches. He talked to people, he watched their reactions, he tried to observe what was going on around him. And sometimes things just fell into place.

It was like working on a jigsaw puzzle. You could look for hours, trying to locate a certain piece to fit a certain spot, and never find it. Then you could leave the table for a while, come back, and see the missing piece immediately. There was no way to explain why the piece had been so hard to find when you were looking for it and so easy to see when you weren't. And then when you fit it into place, the whole puzzle would take shape.

"It started with a couple of feathers," Rhodes said.

He told Ivy about the two feathers he'd picked up at Ty Berry's funeral.

"I thought they were just part of some flower arrangement, but then this afternoon when I drove by Nard King's place, I remembered hearing about the emu business and how it hadn't worked out for a lot of people. Some of them have had so much trouble paying for feed and upkeep that they've just turned the emus loose. Nard's place is run-down, and his emu pens looked empty. So I figured—"

"Hold on," Ivy said. "You mean to tell me that from just a couple of feathers and an empty pen, you came to the conclusion that the ghost was an emu?"

"That's not all," Rhodes said. "When I saw Nard at Rapper's place, I knew he was trying a new way to make money, and I was sure he'd turned his emus loose. He'd rather learn to make drugs than pay for their feed. He was on the shady side from the start, and it's the sort of thing he'd do. I'll have to check, but I wouldn't be surprised if he had the emus insured. If he did, he'll have filed a claim. He might even say they were stolen.''

''And that's it?''

''No,'' Rhodes said. ''What else can move as fast as the ghost does? Remember, I've had a glimpse of it myself. No human being can run that fast, but an emu can. And they're about the right size and shape. Put some teenage kids in a cemetery at night, get an emu on the move, and you've got something that looks a lot like a ghost.''

Ivy thought about it for a while and then said, ''You could be right, I suppose. How are we going to find out?''

''I figured we'd just wait around and see what happens. I don't know much about emus, but I don't think they're nocturnal. Something must be disturbing them and causing them to move around.''

Ivy thought about that, too.

''Trains,'' she said. ''What time does the Amtrak come through?''

Rhodes looked at his watch and said, ''In about fifteen or twenty minutes if it's on time. You think it's the train, then?''

''Why not? Trains make a lot of noise, and there's that flashing light on the engine besides. What else could be stirring them up?''

''I don't know,'' Rhodes said. ''A ghost?''

''You said there wasn't any such thing as ghosts.''

''I might have been lying.''

''In that case, I'd better move over a little closer to

you. We have a few minutes to kill, and maybe you can think of something to do.''

"Maybe," Rhodes said.

THE TRAIN WAS on time. It rattled over the tracks, whistling at every crossing, and its big headlight roved from side to side in front.

"What if it wasn't the train?" Ivy said. "What if it was the wind and the rain and the lightning?"

"We'll find out," Rhodes said.

They sat very still and waited, until the last note of the train's lonesome whistle had faded away into the night and distance. And then they waited some more.

For a long time nothing happened. Then Ivy said, "What's that over there?"

She pointed, and Rhodes looked through the windshield. Something was moving along the fencerow, but it was too dark to tell what it was.

There was a flicker of lightning back in the north, and in a few seconds Rhodes heard a faint crack of thunder.

"That must be our ghost," Rhodes said. "Right on cue. The train woke it up, or scared it."

"Don't you have a spotlight on this car?" Ivy asked.

Rhodes did, and he turned it on, swiveling it by the handle. The light swept across grass and gravestones and obelisks, and then it hit the fence.

The ghost was startled into a run, but Rhodes was able to get a good look at it. It was definitely an emu, a big one, and it was running along the fence faster than Rhodes could follow it with the light. Rhodes knew that if he and Ivy had been outside the car, they'd have heard the grunting sound that emus sometimes made in stressful situations.

Rhodes switched off the light.

"Another mystery solved," he said.

There was more lightning and more thunder. The rain was coming closer.

"You've solved the mystery, all right," Ivy said. "But what about the emus? What are you going to do about them?"

"I'm going to delegate that job."

"Who gets it?"

"Ruth Grady. She's the champion roper of the Sheriff's Department."

"She won't hurt them?"

"Nope. They'll be fine."

"What'll you do with them after she catches them?"

"Maybe somebody will buy them. If not, we'll see if there's a zoo that wants them. You don't have to worry about them. I already have something in mind for them."

"But you're not going to tell me what it is, are you?"

"Not until I see what I can work out."

The first light drops of rain started to pop against the car top and hood.

"What about tonight?" Ivy asked. "Do you have anything worked out for them tonight?"

"A little rain won't hurt them," Rhodes said. "They've been in the rain before. They'll probably get in the trees down by the railroad tracks."

"Good," Ivy said. "Now let's talk about those cats."

THIRTY-FOUR

THE RAIN HUNG AROUND overnight in the form of a dark gray sky and a heavy mist that made the morning air thick and wet and covered everything with tiny droplets of water.

Rhodes went by Faye Knape's house and fed the cats. He still thought of them as Faye's cats, though he was afraid they were well on the way to becoming his. He hadn't quite figured out how he was going to explain things to Speedo and Yancey. Maybe, he thought, he wouldn't have to. Maybe the Knape heirs wouldn't want the cats to go to anyone in law enforcement. Maybe they had some adoptive parents in mind already.

Fat chance, he thought.

The cats were glad to see him, but only because he was feeding them. They hadn't suddenly developed an undying affection for him overnight.

He gave them food and fresh water and left. For some reason, his eyes weren't itching nearly as much as they should have been, and he sneezed only once on the way to his car.

Melva Keeler was standing out on her porch in her robe and fuzzy slippers. She was holding her morning newspaper and looking across the street through the mist.

Rhodes wiped water off his face and thought about going over and talking to her, just to see if she'd break down and confess to Faye's murder, but that would have to wait. He had other things on his mind.

When he got to the jail, he told Hack that the cemetery

ghosts were as good as broken. Or busted, or caught. Whichever Hack preferred. He told him to send Ruth Grady out with her lasso to round them up.

"There are probably two of them," Rhodes said. "Maybe more. She'll have to hunt them down."

"Hunt what down?" Hack said. "What're you talkin' about?"

Lawton was there, too, getting ready to do his morning count of the prisoners.

"Yeah," he said. "What're you talkin' about?"

Rhodes could have given them an even bigger dose of their own medicine, but he didn't have time for it. So he told them about the emus.

"Dang," Hack said. "I gotta hand it to you, Sheriff. I never would've thought of that. Are you sure that's what the ghosts are?"

"I'm sure," Rhodes said. "I saw one of them last night. Ivy saw it, too."

"I guess if Ivy saw it, that cinches it," Lawton said. "There's just one little problem, though."

"Problem?" Rhodes said.

"Yeah. If that was an emu out there in the cemetery, what was in here? It wasn't any emu, I can tell you that. Our security might not be as tight as in a big city jail, but it's tight enough to keep a six-foot-tall bird out."

"Has anybody seen a ghost in here since there was one reported out in the cemetery?" Rhodes asked.

"No," Lawton said.

"And who's going to tell the prisoners that we know what the one out there is?"

"Oh," Lawton said. "Not me. What about you, Hack?"

"Not me. I don't like ghosts hangin' around where I'm tryin' to do my work."

"So as long as they think the ghost is in the cemetery, we don't have to worry," Rhodes said. "Right?"

"Right," Hack said, and Lawton echoed him.

"So that just leaves one thing to worry about," Hack said.

"What now?" Rhodes asked.

"Those emus. How's Ruth gonna haul 'em anywhere? She can't use the county car. They'll make a mess of it."

"Couldn't be worse than some of the drunks she brings in," Lawton said. "You ever smell the car after one of them's heaved in the back seat? Lordy mercy."

"She won't have to bring them in a car," Rhodes said. "Hack, you call one of the commissioners, Purcell will do, and tell him we need a truck and trailer. And someone to help Ruth load the emus. That'll take care of it."

"I guess you're right," Hack said. "We could use an animal control officer around here."

"No money," Rhodes said. "After you call Purcell, get in touch with Buddy. He and I are going to visit the Packers."

"You gonna pick them up for stealin' and drug makin'?" Hack asked.

"We can't prove a thing on the drug charge. But the stealing, well, that's another story."

"What about Nard King?"

"We're not going to arrest him. I have something else in mind."

"You want to let me know what it is?"

"He's going back into the emu business," Rhodes said.

RHODES WENT BY the office of Jack Parry, the county judge, and got a search warrant. This time he was going to be fully prepared. Then he went back by the jail for Buddy, and they drove to Obert.

Their first stop was at Nard's house. Rhodes drove into the yard, and Buddy pulled in behind him. Nard's pickup wasn't there. Rhodes went to the house and knocked. No one answered. It was clear that there was no one at home.

"You think he's skipped?" Buddy asked.

Rhodes considered that idea.

"No," he said. "But I think we'd better be even more prepared for the Packers than we thought."

"Why? What's going on?"

"It just occurred to me that maybe there's a tuition refund after all."

Buddy didn't get it. "Tuition refund?"

"Call it a makeup class. Rapper didn't give the Packers their money back, but he might agree to teach them what they wanted to know, as long as they provided the classroom."

"You think they'd be crazy enough to do it at their place?"

"They might. They have plenty of houses to do it in if you count the mobile homes."

"They've got guns, right?"

"Plenty of them," Rhodes said.

"Doesn't bother me," Buddy said. "You think Rapper'll blow things up again?"

"I don't think the Packers would let him."

"Let's hope you're right," Buddy said.

RHODES DIDN'T SEE ANY motorcycles when he drove into the Packers' yard, but there were a couple of pickups that hadn't been there the day before.

Buddy came along behind Rhodes and blocked off the entrance, though Rhodes didn't think that would help.

The Packers would know about other ways to get out, and so would Rapper. He was no Eckstine, but he'd fooled Rhodes more than once. He was the kind of guy who'd just as soon leave by the back door as the front. Maybe he'd rather.

Rhodes got out of his car and waited for Buddy to join him. There were pools of muddy water standing in the yard, and the chickens looked more bedraggled than ever in the dense mist, though it didn't stop them from pecking around in the mud for whatever it was they found there.

Buddy walked up and stood beside Rhodes.

"Where do you think Rapper and his students are?" the deputy asked.

"Not in any of these places," Rhodes said, looking at the mobile home. Drops of water slid down its rusty sides. "There's another mobile home shell just over the hill in that field behind the house. I'd guess that's where they are. If they're anywhere."

"Think we should check the house, just in case?"

"Wouldn't hurt. You go ahead."

While Buddy was knocking on the door, Rhodes walked on toward the back. The ruts that he and Ruth had seen on their previous visit were still there, but they were cut deeper into the mud. Rhodes didn't want to try driving the county car along them for fear of getting stuck in the mud. He went back to the car and got the shotgun.

After a minute or so, Buddy came out to the car, shaking his head.

"Find anyone?" Rhodes asked.

"Just a kid," Buddy said. "He told me there was no one else there, but I think he was lying. I could hear the TV going. Sounded like *The Jerry Springer Show*, judging from all the yelling that was going on."

Rhodes wouldn't have expected the Packers to be watching PBS.

"They probably told the boy what to tell you," Rhodes said. "Anyway, I think the people we want will be back in the field."

"Think I need my shotgun?"

"It might be a good idea."

Buddy got his shotgun, and the two of them walked around the house and followed the ruts up the hill. The ground was squishy under Rhodes's shoes, and the wet weeds brushed his pants legs, which kept getting heavier as he walked along and more water soaked into them. Rhodes brushed his hand across his hair. It was as if he'd been standing under a shower.

"You oughta get you a hat," Buddy said.

Buddy wore a hat day and night, and today he'd put a clear plastic cover on it to keep off the dampness. Drops of water stood up on it as if it were a freshly waxed car. Buddy wasn't going to have water spots on his Stetson.

"Hats bother me," Rhodes said.

"Keep your hair dry, though," Buddy said.

They went through the gap in the fence and stood looking down the hill to where the mobile home sat. There were two motorcycles and a blue pickup parked behind it.

"That Nard King's truck?" Buddy asked.

"Looks like it."

Buddy hefted his shotgun.

"How many of them do you think there are?"

"I'd guess six or seven," Rhodes said. "No more than eight at the most."

"Gonna be pretty hard for you and me to surround that place. We should've brought Ruth with us."

"You're probably right," Rhodes said. "But she's busy rounding up emus."

"We gonna try to sneak up on them?"

"I don't think they'll be expecting us. But it might be a good idea to be quiet and careful."

"Quiet and careful are my middle names," Buddy said.

Then he took two steps forward, stepped into a hole that had been dug by a nesting rabbit or a passing armadillo, and loosed off a shotgun blast that reverberated across the wet field and shook the mist out of the air like rain.

THIRTY-FIVE

THERE WAS A MOMENT of total silence after the shotgun's roar. It was as if the world had come to a complete stop and was waiting for some signal to put it back into motion.

"Dadgum it," Buddy said, and things started to move again.

Rhodes rushed toward the mobile home, mounted the concrete step in front of the door, and raised his foot.

"Sheriff's Department!" he yelled, and kicked the flimsy door in.

The door flew back and hit the wall inside, but by that time Rhodes was sitting on the ground beside the step, which was just as well. Otherwise he would have been hit by one or more of the bullets that zipped through the open doorway.

Rhodes motioned for Buddy to go around back. Buddy was up and running, but he was too late. Rhodes heard glass shatter, and he knew that Rapper would be on his way out.

Rhodes stood up and fired his shotgun upward through the door. He wasn't trying to hit anyone, just let them know that he was about to come through. Now that they'd had a second to think about it, maybe they'd hold their fire. They wouldn't want to kill an officer of the law.

Or maybe they would, though Rhodes didn't really think so.

He heard motorcycles thunder to life, and then he heard Buddy yell, "Freeze!"

Nobody froze. Nobody ever did. Buddy fired his shotgun.

When he did, Rhodes jumped through the door of the mobile home, turning in midair and sliding in on his back. He fired the shotgun left and right, straight up at the ceiling, before his head hit the wall. The pellets ripped through the cheap ceiling tile and tore through the metal roof.

Rhodes jumped up, waving away the acrid smoke with one hand, but he didn't see a single soul. They'd all gone out through the sliding glass door on the back, though they hadn't bothered to slide it.

Rhodes stepped through the door and down into the field. There were Packers running in all directions. They were all armed, but none of them was taking the time to shoot. One of them looked like an explosion in a hair factory, and Rhodes recognized him from the cemetery. He recognized Dude, too, and Ferrell. He was sure he could make a case against them when the time came.

Rapper and Nellie had almost reached the trees along the creek on their motorcycles. Mud was spraying up from beneath their rear tires.

Buddy was standing rigidly by Nard King's pickup, holding his shotgun about a foot away from King's left ear. King had his hands clasped in back of his neck. He looked like a man who'd just lost his last dollar and been told his dog had died.

Rhodes ran over to the pickup and opened the door. The keys were in the ignition, ready to help someone make a quick getaway. Rhodes put the shotgun in the seat, got in himself, and started the pickup.

"I'll be back," he told Buddy. "Don't let King get away."

Buddy made some kind of answer, but Rhodes didn't hear it. He was already swerving down the hill, the pickup's tires sliding first one way and then the other over the slick, muddy ground.

"Don't let me get stuck," Rhodes said aloud, turning on the windshield wipers and bouncing around in the truck cab like a BB in a bucket. He fought the steering wheel as it spun under his hands.

He was fifty yards behind the motorcycles when they disappeared into the trees. He figured that Rapper and Nellie would go in different directions, and the one he wanted was Rapper. Which way would he go, right or left?

Rhodes drove into the trees. Their limbs slapped at the windshield and obscured his vision. Then one of them grabbed the left wiper and ripped it off the truck. Rhodes wondered if Nard had insurance, not that he really cared.

He made a left turn along the creek bank, heading away from the deep hole where the Packers had tried to hide their Dodge Ram. Somehow the left turn seemed easier to Rhodes, and he hoped it had seemed the same to Rapper. Either Rapper or Nellie had made the turn, Rhodes knew, because he could see the ruts cut by the motorcycle wheels.

The going along the side of the creek wasn't easy, but it was easier for Rhodes than for whoever was on the motorcycle. Rhodes crushed bushes under the pickup's tires and bulled his way right over small trees. Once he nearly slid into the creek, but he managed to jerk the wheel in the right direction and save himself.

After what seemed like forever but was probably more like thirty seconds, Rhodes spotted a motorcycle lying on its side right at the edge of the creek bank, its back wheel hanging over the lip of the bank and still spinning. There was a long skid mark leading up to the motorcycle, but there was no sign of its rider.

Rhodes stopped the truck and got out. The woods were no place for a shotgun, so he drew his pistol and walked over to the motorcycle. Its rider had made clear tracks in the mud and leaves leading away from it into the trees.

Rhodes followed the tracks cautiously. Nellie wouldn't be a problem, but Rapper was another story. Rapper would figure out some way to trick Rhodes if he could. And he could. Rhodes was just hoping it wouldn't happen again.

Moisture slid off tree leaves like rain and plopped on Rhodes's head. Mud and fallen leaves stuck to his shoes, which got heavier with every step he took. It became more difficult to follow the tracks because whoever had made them was being careful to step on the hardest ground, on rocks, on piles of leaves. Finally Rhodes lost the trail entirely.

More than once Rhodes had found himself in similar situations, following someone in the woods. He remembered a time when he'd been looking so carefully behind every tree that the man he'd been after had jumped on him from above. Rapper didn't look like a tree climber, but Rhodes couldn't take the chance that he wasn't. He scanned the lower branches as he went along but saw no one.

He kept walking until he saw off to his right the thick trunk of an old tree that had been blown over in some storm, taking a couple of smaller trees down with it. Its tangled roots stood at least five feet high. They were embedded with dark mud and dirt, and a green vine was growing near the top.

Rhodes thought the trunk and roots would provide a perfect hiding place. Rapper could be lying beside the trunk or crouched behind the roots, and Rhodes approached warily. He was almost to the huge mass of roots when he saw footprints just in front of him. Someone had been in a hurry and slipped in the mud. The footprints pointed to the left, away from the tree. Looking in that direction, Rhodes saw a dense tangle of vines and brush, another good hiding place.

He turned and started toward it, careful not to make a sound, though if Rapper was hiding there he could surely see Rhodes coming.

When Rhodes was about halfway there, he heard something behind him. It wasn't much of a noise, the faintest scuff of a shoe on wet leaves, but it was enough to make Rhodes realize that Rapper had fooled him one more time.

Rhodes turned as quickly as he could, knowing all along that he was going to be too late.

Rapper had given up on being quiet and was charging Rhodes like a rogue rhino, covering the ground between them much more rapidly than Rhodes would have thought possible for a man with a serious limp.

The biker ran awkwardly and heavily, but he was fast. What made his speed even more remarkable was that he was holding a large tree limb over his head with both hands, a limb that could crush Rhodes's skull like a cheap light bulb.

Rhodes backpedaled clumsily and brought up his pistol, hoping to get off a warning shot and distract Rapper, but his feet slipped out from under him and the pistol went off.

As he fell, Rhodes saw the side of Rapper's head explode in a pink haze of blood.

THIRTY-SIX

RHODES HIT THE GROUND, sick and hollow inside. He had never killed anyone before, never wanted to, never intended to. Not even Rapper, who, Rhodes suddenly noticed, was proving remarkably active for a dead man.

He was holding his right hand tight to the side of his head and bellowing like a wounded walrus, blood running between his fingers. He took his hand away, and Rhodes saw the ragged remains of Rapper's right ear. It looked as if the entire top half of it had been shot away, and blood flowed freely from what was left.

Rhodes had always heard that wounds to the scalp and ear bleed more profusely than those to other parts of the body. He believed it.

Rapper put his hand back against his head and glared at Rhodes where he lay on the muddy ground. The look in his eyes was pure malevolence. Rhodes tightened his finger on the trigger of his pistol, but Rapper wasn't going to take anymore chances with him. He ran off, heading back toward where his motorcycle lay on the creek bank.

Rhodes was too shaken to try to stop him. He lay where he was for a full minute before getting to his feet. He brushed wet leaves from his pants and shirt, but he didn't bother trying to get rid of the mud that stuck wetly to him. He knew that brushing it would just smear it.

He walked back through the woods. Rapper's motorcycle was gone. Rhodes hadn't even heard it start. He figured Rapper would join Nellie and the two of them would be long gone. Unless Rapper bled to death first. Rhodes didn't think there was much danger of that, no matter how serious the wound had seemed. It was only an ear, after all.

Rhodes slogged over to Nard King's pickup, and when he finally got it turned around, he drove it back up the hill to where Buddy and Nard were waiting.

RUTH MET RHODES, Buddy, and Nard at Nard's house. She was driving a white Ford pickup with a county emblem painted in blue on the doors and pulling a cattle trailer. There were four emus in the trailer.

Ruth stuck her head out of the truck window and said, "Hack told me you'd found a home for these birds and sent me out here. Is this the place?"

"This is it," Rhodes said. "I think the birds will recognize it."

"I never saw those birds before in my life," Nard said. "They didn't come from here."

"Give it up, Nard," Rhodes said. "You know they belong to you. And if you had enough money to pay Rapper for that drug class, you can afford to feed these emus."

"Drug class? I don't know what you're talking about. We were just having a friendly poker game."

"Gambling's illegal, too," Buddy said.

"We were playing for matchsticks."

Rhodes laughed. He had to hand it to Nard, who had more nerve that Rhodes would've thought.

"We did find a few matchsticks when we searched that trailer," he said.

He and Buddy had cuffed King and put him in the pickup bed while they searched the mobile home. Unfortunately, their earlier arrival had interrupted Rapper and the Packers before any drug making had begun. Rapper and Nellie must have been organizing their materials. If the whole bunch of them hadn't panicked and run, he and Buddy might have been able to brazen their way through things. But the Packers had been too worried about what Rhodes might do to them because of their nocturnal activities to hang around.

"Sure there were matchsticks," Nard said. "That's because of the poker. There was nothing else in there except for what they call in the papers your 'common household items.'"

That was true.

"And of course no one was going to use those common household items to make an illegal drug," Rhodes said.

"I can't be responsible for what some of those old boys might've been doing in another room," Nard said. "I was playing cards."

"You stick to that," Rhodes said. "In fact, I might even believe you."

Nard's mouth dropped open. "You might?"

"Under certain conditions," Rhodes said.

Nard tried to look shrewd, failed, and said, "What conditions?"

"That these emus get the best care you can give them from here on in. That you don't ever let them out again."

"But they're a losing proposition!" Nard said. "Not that they're mine or that I ever let them out."

"I'll be checking by here pretty often," Rhodes said. "Or one of the deputies will. They'll want to be sure everything's all right."

"How can I ever make any money on those damn things?" Nard whined.

"That's your problem. Of course, if you don't want to

do it, I can arrange to solve all your problems for you. I can get you free room, board, and a nice orange polyester jumpsuit to wear."

Nard stood there for a second or two and then said, "I'll take care of them, then. What about my truck?"

"Deputy Reynolds will take you back to get it, now that we've got your promise."

"That's not what I mean!"

"What, then?"

"You just about ruined it! Who's gonna pay for that?"

"Call your insurance company," Rhodes said. "Ruth, back that trailer up to the emu pens, and let's get them unloaded."

"YOU LOOK LIKE you been wrestlin' hogs," Hack said when Rhodes came through the jail door.

"Mud wrestlin'," Lawton said. "That's pretty eighties if you ask me."

Rhodes didn't feel like discussing his appearance, so he ignored them.

"What about the emus?" Hack asked.

"You don't have to worry about them," Rhodes told him. "Nard King's decided that he wants to take care of them."

"I thought he was the one that turned 'em out," Lawton said.

"He is. But he's had a change of heart."

"It's a real comfort when that happens," Hack said. "Just goes to show you that people can turn their lives around in the right direction if you just give 'em a chance. I don't guess Rapper and Nellie did the same."

"No," Rhodes said. "They got away. But Rapper has something to remember us by."

He told them about shooting Rapper's ear off, with a couple of embellishments.

"That's some real marksmanship," Lawton said when Rhodes had finished the story. "I'd say you were cuttin' it mighty close, though. It's a wonder you didn't kill him."

"We skilled pistoleers can do all kinds of things," Rhodes said. "I could probably shoot a cigarette out of your mouth if I tried. Want to see?"

"I don't smoke," Lawton said. "Thanks anyway. I'll just take your word for it."

"Me, too," Hack said. "With Rapper and Nellie gone, that just leaves the Packers. What're you gonna do about them?"

"They're probably hiding out with some of their relatives outside the county," Rhodes said. "They'll stay out of sight for a few weeks and then come sneaking back when they think I've forgotten about them."

"They don't know you very well if they think you'll forget," Hack said. "Not to change the subject, but Faye Knape's son is in town. The daughter won't get in till later on. The son's already called Jack Parry, and he's not one bit happy."

"Who's *he?*" Rhodes asked.

"The son, but Jack Parry's not exactly cheerful, either. You know how much politicians like it when somebody jumps on 'em, even if the somebody's not a local voter."

"I don't guess anybody mentioned the cats."

"Jack Parry did. Said he could hear 'em yowlin' in the background when he was on the phone. They don't like Miz Knape's son one bit, is what he said."

Rhodes said he doubted that Parry had said anything of the kind.

"Maybe not, but he would've if he'd thought about it.

Lawton and I both think it's your Christian duty to take care of those cats."

Rhodes gave them a level look.

"Thanks for sharing that with me," he said.

THIRTY-SEVEN

RHODES WENT HOME to change clothes. He had to hop around the room on one foot while he was taking his pants off because Yancey was on the attack.

"If I brought those cats home, it would serve you right," Rhodes told him.

Yancey stopped yipping and sat on his haunches, looking up expectantly.

"Got your attention, huh?" Rhodes said, taking advantage of the opportunity to get his pants off and into the washing machine. "Good. I'm talking cats here, Yancey. Three of them. One of them's as big as you are."

Yancey cocked his head and perked his ears.

"Maybe bigger," Rhodes went on. "And you know how cats are. They sleep in the chairs, they climb on the table, they sneak a snack from the dog's bowl now and then."

Yancey gave a low growl, or as low as he could go. It wouldn't have struck fear into even the most timid of cats.

"You sound like you're looking forward to meeting them," Rhodes said. "Serve you right, is what I say. Ivy wants to adopt them, but I'm hoping their current owners won't want to give them to the likes of an incompetent lawman like me."

Yancey turned and walked away, no longer interested in the conversation, and Rhodes got his clothes changed. Before he left, he went out to the mailbox to see if there was any good news. There never was, but he continued to hope that Ed McMahon would somehow make a mistake and declare him a winner in that sweepstakes he advertised. It was a faint hope, since Rhodes never entered, but he'd heard that his chances of winning were about the same whether he entered or not.

He opened the mailbox and pulled out a Wal-Mart circular, a credit card bill, and a catalog from the Sportsman's Friend. He flipped through the catalog, looking at tents and reproductions of famous firearms. So much for Ed McMahon.

Rhodes took the mail back inside and laid it on the kitchen table. Yancey lay under a chair and watched him.

"Are you sick?" Rhodes asked. "Or just thinking about those cats?"

Yancey didn't answer, and Rhodes went out back to roughhouse with Speedo for a few minutes. When they were both tired of the game, Rhodes stood up, and all the puzzle pieces seemed to fall into place in Rhodes's head.

He got in the county car and headed for Melva Keeler's house.

THE SUN WAS TRYING to break through the clouds and mist, giving the day an oddly gray brightness. The air was practically tropical, and the streets were slick with moisture.

Rhodes parked in front of Melva Keeler's place and looked over at the Knape house. There was a car parked in the driveway, partially concealed by bushes. Rhodes figured the car belonged to the son.

He knocked on Melva's door, and she came to greet him in her usual outfit: robe and fuzzy slippers. She was holding a thick coffee mug in one hand.

"Good afternoon, Sheriff," she said. "I was just having some coffee. Would you like a cup?"

One of Rhodes's peculiarities was that he didn't drink coffee, not in the afternoon, not in the evening, not even in the mornings with breakfast. The thought of breakfast reminded Rhodes that he'd missed lunch again. He wondered if Melva had any Vienna sausages. Probably not.

"No, thanks," he said. "I'd like to ask you a few questions, though. Can I come in?"

"Of course. Be my guest."

Melva stepped back and opened the door. Rhodes went inside, where he found himself in a darkened hallway. All the shades in the house were drawn, and it was as dank as a cave.

"The light bothers my eyes," Melva explained. "Come along. We can talk in the den."

Rhodes's shoe soles squeaked on the hardwood floor as he followed her to a sparsely furnished room where a small black and white TV set was flickering. Alex Trebek was waiting for someone to give him a question for the answer *1066*. Rhodes wondered if anyone could give a question for A.D. 11. Aside from the TV set, the only light in the room came from a floor lamp with a twenty-five-watt bulb and an imitation Tiffany shade. Melva turned down the sound on the TV set, and she and Rhodes sat in straight-backed wooden chairs with wooden bottoms.

"If you're wondering how I saw Vernell the other day," Melva said, "it's because I just happened to be out on the porch at the time. I like to go out for a breath of air now and then."

Rhodes didn't blame her. If he lived in a place like this, he'd go out now and then, too. Probably more often than just now and then.

"Have you caught whoever killed poor Faye?" Melva asked.

"That's what I'm here about," Rhodes said. "Maybe you can help me."

"My word, Sheriff. I don't see how I can do that. I've told you all I know about it."

"I don't think so," Rhodes said.

Melva leaned back as far as she could in her chair, which wasn't very far.

"If there's something I haven't told you," she said, "I don't know what it is. Are you going to give me a hint?"

"It's about Faye's husband," Rhodes said. "And his guns. Do you remember the guns?"

"Well, yes, but not very well. As I think I told you, I visited Faye now and then, but we weren't exactly close friends."

"You knew they were there, though."

"Yes. I don't know much about guns, Sheriff."

"You probably know enough about them to know that if you killed someone with one of them, you should get rid of it, don't you?"

"I watch television, if that's what you mean."

Rhodes thought about *Murder, She Wrote*. Watching it hadn't helped Faye Knape.

He said, "And if you wanted someone to think another person had committed a murder, you'd probably know enough to plant the gun on that other person, wouldn't you?"

"I'm not sure I've seen that on television. Do you watch a lot of television, Sheriff?"

"Not nearly enough," Rhodes said.

"I'm sorry."

"Me, too. Now, about those guns."

"What about them?"

"When was the last time you saw them?"

"My word, Sheriff. I don't have any idea."

"Think about it," Rhodes said.

Melva looked at the TV set, where one of the *Jeopardy* contestants had just missed a Daily Double and lost everything. Then she looked back at Rhodes.

"It must have been recently," she said finally. "Maybe the last time I was over there."

"So you didn't know she'd sold them?"

"Why, no. She never mentioned that to me. Is it important?"

"It might be," Rhodes said.

THIRTY-EIGHT

WHEN RHODES WALKED into the antique store, Richard Rascoe was sitting in the barber chair reading a copy of the *Antique Trader* and looking natty in a camel-colored jacket and a tie with Disney characters on it.

"What can I do for you, Sheriff?" he asked.

"Show me some guns," Rhodes said.

"Guns?" Rascoe let the *Trader* fall into his lap and looked around his store. "I don't sell guns."

"Not here in Thurston, maybe, but you sell them. Faye Knape sold her husband's collection to you. I found the bill of sale at her house."

"There wasn't any" Rascoe paused, realizing his mistake. "I don't know what you're talking about, Sheriff."

"Murder," Rhodes said. "You killed Ty Berry and Faye Knape. I have a warrant for your arrest."

"You must be crazy," Rascoe said.

"There are people who'd agree with you about that," Rhodes said, remembering that Faye Knape had said the same thing. "But in this case they'd be wrong. I know about the angel. I know you met Berry in the cemetery and killed him. I know you killed Faye Knape and left one of her husband's pistols in the house for me to find. You confused the issue, but it just didn't work out for you."

Rascoe tried a smile, but it kept sliding off his face.

"I still don't know what you're talking about," he said.

"Your first mistake," Rhodes said, "was taking the

catalog from Faye's house. I didn't think about it until today, when I got a catalog in the mail. After I showed Faye Knape that catalog with the angel in it, I left it at her house. But it was gone when I searched the place."

"She must have thrown it away," Rascoe said.

"I don't think so. I think you took it. Or maybe not. She came to see you the day you killed her, and maybe she brought the catalog with her. She already knew what it's taken me way too long to figure out."

"I don't want to listen to anymore of this," Rascoe said. "Please leave my store. A customer might come in. I don't want anyone to hear these false accusations."

"I don't think you have a lot of customers in this store," Rhodes said. "I think you have other ways of making your money. And the accusations aren't false. Everything was in plain sight, but I just didn't see it, mainly because I believed you instead of Faye. I thought she'd made a mistake, but she knew she hadn't. The angel she saw was one that had been stolen, all right, and Ty Berry knew it, too. I don't know why he didn't come to me about it. Maybe you told him you'd investigate it and find out where it came from. Anything to buy you the time to order one from Benson's Concrete Works to replace it with."

"You can't prove any of this," Rascoe said. "It's all speculation, and it's all wrong."

"I doubt it," Rhodes said. "If it's wrong, it's not wrong by much. I think you set Ty up. I think you told him that you'd found out who'd stolen the angel and that you had information they were planning another theft in the Clearview Cemetery. You two would meet and put a stop to it, since my office wasn't doing anything. He even left a note about it. 'A.D. Eleven.' At first I thought it was a date, but it was just initials and a time. 'Antique Dealer at eleven o'clock' is what it meant.''

"You're just guessing," Rascoe said.

"Maybe. Maybe not. I think you met him and shot him with a .22 derringer you bought from Faye Knape, then left it in her house after you killed her. You probably gave her the same line you gave Ty, told her you'd see what you could find out, then met her later and killed her. You should've put the pistol back in the gun cabinet instead of in that drawer, though."

"Sheriff, all that's very interesting, but it doesn't have a thing to do with me. It's all so flimsy that a puff of wind would blow it to Canada."

"I have more," Rhodes said. "I have the Packers."

"The Packers?"

"Sure. Not the football team. The people who've been stealing for you. I should have figured that out sooner, too. The Packers will steal and poach and maybe even sell drugs, but they wouldn't know a thing about how to sell cemetery artifacts. They'd need someone to do that for them, someone like you. That kind of thing brings big money in some places. New Orleans, for example. In fact, I expect you went to the Packers with the idea. They'll tell me, eventually."

Rhodes figured that the Packers were the weak link in the whole scheme. Once he put them under arrest, which he would as soon as they came back into the county, they'd confess to anything to save their own necks. Rhodes would have to visit Marlee, tell her he was ready to cut a deal, and have her get in touch with the rest of the clan. Sooner or later, they'd come home. They always did.

"Maybe your fingerprints are on the gun, too," Rhodes said.

Rascoe didn't say a word. He reached out his right hand and grabbed the pole of the heavy traffic signal in the corner. With a hard pull, he smashed it into Rhodes's side.

Rhodes managed to dodge, but not quite in time. The light hit him, and he stumbled sideways and into the quilt rack, which collapsed under his weight. He went down in a welter of patchwork.

Before he could get up, Rascoe threw a bunny-covered teapot at him. Rhodes got an arm in the way, and the teapot glanced off to one side, shattering into fragments when it hit the floor.

Rhodes tried to get up again, but this time Rascoe pushed a bookcase over on him. Dusty books pelted him, and one of the shelves hit him in the head. He sprawled under the bookcase, and Rascoe ran out the front door.

Rhodes raised up, pushed the bookcase off his back, and went out after Rascoe. He didn't have to go far. Rascoe was practically next door.

Hob Barrett was standing in front of his store with one hand clutching the collar of Rascoe's natty sport coat and the other holding the Disney tie. Rascoe was struggling, waving his arms and kicking, but it wasn't doing him any good. When Hob Barrett clamped down on something, he didn't let go.

"You lookin' for this character, Sheriff?" Barrett asked. "I saw you go in his place, so I figured if he was runnin' from anything, it must be you."

"Thanks, Hob," Rhodes said. "Hold him still while I get these handcuffs on him."

After Rascoe was safely stowed in the county car, Barrett said, "Anything else I can do for you, Sheriff?"

"How about a can of Vienna sausage?" Rhodes said.

THIRTY-NINE

"WELL," HACK SAID, "you got the ghosts busted, you got the cemetery robberies stopped, and you solved the murders. Not a bad job."

Rhodes was looking through the papers on his desk, trying to find his reading glasses. He didn't even bother to look around. He knew what was coming.

"Don't know what you'd have done, though, if those Packers hadn't come through for you," Hack went on, not at all bothered by the fact that Rhodes was ignoring him.

"He knew they'd come through," Lawton said. He was leaning against the doorframe, one leg bent, his foot against the wall. "He knew they'd rather rat out their buddy than go to jail on drug charges."

"Couldn't have made those stick anyway," Hack said. "But we got 'em tied down tight on the cemetery jobs."

"Should've known better'n to try sinking that stuff in the creek along with their truck," Lawton said. "Should've known we'd go in and get it out."

Rhodes was tempted to say he hadn't seen either Hack or Lawton wading out in the creek, knee-deep in slimy mud, to get anything out of the Packers' truck. But he kept quiet. He found his reading glasses and put them on.

"Got some good TV coverage out of it, too," Hack said. "By the time those fellas in Dallas got organized and came down here, everything was tied up in a neat bow. You like the way you looked on the TV, Sheriff?"

Rhodes finally turned around, looking at them over the tops of his glasses because he knew that irritated them.

"The camera adds ten pounds," he said.

"Yeah," Hack agreed. "I noticed that double chin."

Rhodes didn't want to talk about his double chin, which he thought was merely a figment of the camera's imagination in the first place. He turned back to his desk.

"Bad thing is, you didn't get Rapper and Nellie," Lawton said.

"'Dey'll be beck,'" Hack said, sounding like Arnold Schwarzenegger might have sounded if he'd lived in Texas all his life. "One of these days, Rapper'll want to find the rest of his ear."

"What worries me is those poor little kitty-cats," Lawton said, pushing himself away from the doorframe. "Likely they'll starve to death before long."

"Starve for affection, too," Hack added.

Rhodes turned around again, looked over the top of his glasses.

"The cats will be just fine," he said. "I've made arrangements for them."

"What arrangements?" Hack asked. "You didn't say anything to us about any arrangements."

"I'm going by this afternoon to pick them up," Rhodes said. "Someone's adopting them."

Hack and Lawton looked at each other, then looked at Rhodes.

"Nobody told us," Hack said.

"You didn't ask."

"I'm askin' now. Who's gonna adopt those cats? You?"

"No," Rhodes said, enjoying himself. "But I could if I wanted to."

"I thought you were allergic," Lawton said.

"I might be, but Ivy thinks I might have been more allergic to Faye Knape's perfume than to her cats. She could be right. But now I don't have to find out."

"Well, if you aren't adoptin' 'em, who is?" Hack asked.

"Melva Keeler," Rhodes said. "She needs some company in that old house of hers. Those cats will be perfect. They won't have to move far, and Faye's son approves."

The telephone rang, and Hack answered. He listened, then said, "Someone'll be right there."

He hung up and turned to Rhodes.

"Shirley, Goodness, and Mercy are on the loose again, or at least two of 'em are. Somebody's gonna have to round 'em up."

"Call Ruth," Rhodes said. "She's got her lasso."

"This is her day off," Hack said. He opened his desk drawer. "But she left this here, just in case."

He pulled a coiled rope out of the drawer.

Rhodes sighed.

"Don't take it so hard," Hack said. "Maybe Vernell can write a book about you."

"Or use your picture on the cover," Lawton said. "You could be just like Terry Don Coslin."

Rhodes got up and took the rope from Hack, thinking about the way the TV camera had given him a double chin.

"That'll be the day," he said.

MARY LOGUE

DARK
COULEE

A CLAIRE WATKINS MYSTERY

Though life in rural Wisconsin is having some healing
effects for ex-Minneapolis cop Claire Watkins, she is
still plagued by nightmares of past tragedy. Now
she's plunged into a shattering murder case that will
force her to confront the demons that still haunt her.

Widower Jeb Spitzer is knifed to death at the local
harvest moon dance, leaving three teenagers orphaned.
But Claire senses a feeling of desperate relief
among the three kids. As she peels back
the layers of the crime, she uncovers a
shocking connection to Spitzer's wife's
"accidental" death, and secrets that
premeditated both incidents.

Available October 2001
at your favorite retail outlet.

 WORLDWIDE LIBRARY®

WML398

Kathleen Anne Barrett

Milwaukee
Autumns Can Be
LETHAL

A BETH HARTLEY MYSTERY

Lawyer turned legal researcher and amateur
sleuth, Beth Hartley is hired to do some
work for an old law school acquaintance,
Don Balstrum. But when she finds Don
murdered in his office, her meticulous
mind for details leads her immediately
on the path of a complex crime.

With her tenacity and insight into
the legal profession, she soon opens
many dark doors into Don's world: his
unforgiving father, his antagonistic twin
brother, his cagey business partners and
his ex-wife—all with secrets to hide.

Available October 2001 at your favorite retail outlet.

WKAB399

Camille Minichino

The Beryllium Murder

A GLORIA LAMERINO MYSTERY

Physicist-sleuth Gloria Lamerino heads back
to her old stomping grounds in Berkeley,
California, to look into the death of a former
colleague, Gary Larkin, dead of beryllium
poisoning. Though his death has been ruled
accidental, Gloria is suspicious: Gary was much
too aware of the hazards of this dangerous
element to be so reckless in his handling of it.

The pieces of the puzzle come together like
a new molecular formula for homicide:
Internet pornography, hacking, extortion,
jealousy and revenge—and a killer making
murder into a science.

"It's a good thing the periodic table is big
enough for 100 more adventures."
—Janet Evanovich, author of *Hot Six*

*Available October 2001
at your favorite retail outlet.*

Take 2 books and a surprise gift FREE!

SPECIAL LIMITED-TIME OFFER

MURDER, MAYHEM *And* MISTLETOE

Terence Faherty, Aileen Schumacher, Wendi Lee, Bill Crider

Four new tales of Christmas crimes from four of today's most popular mystery writers.

THE HEADLESS MAGI

What do several alarming calls to a crisis center and vandalism at a local nativity scene have in common? Owen Keane, metaphysical sleuth in Terence Faherty's Edgar-nominated series is about to find out!

CHRISTMAS CACHE

Aileen Schumacher's New Mexico sleuth, Tory Travers, finds herself undertaking a challenging Christmas puzzle: an international network of art thieves, a backyard full of cash, and a mysterious shooting.

STOCKING STUFFER

Wendi Lee's Boston P.I. Angela Matelli uncovers a case of shoplifting that leads to murder…

THE EMPTY MANGER

Bill Crider's easygoing Texas sheriff Dan Rhodes has his hands full with a "living" manger scene in downtown Clearview, especially when the body of the local councilwoman is found dead behind it.

Available November 2001
at your favorite retail outlet.

 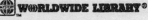 **WORLDWIDE LIBRARY** ®

WMMM

Enjoy the mystery and suspense of

POISON APPLES

NANCY MEANS WRIGHT

A VERMONT MYSTERY

"Wright's most gripping and satisfying mystery to date."
—*Female Detective*

"...Wright doesn't put a foot wrong in this well-wrought mystery."
—*Boston Globe*

After tragedy shatters Moira and Stan Earthrowl's lives, running an apple orchard in Vermont gives them a chance to heal. Yet their newfound idyll is short-lived as "accidents" begin to plague the massive orchard: tractor brakes fail, apples are poisoned.

Desperate, Moira turns to neighbor Ruth Willmarth for help. Ruth's investigation reveals a list of possible saboteurs, including a fanatical religious cult and a savvy land developer who, ironically, is Ruth's ex-husband. But deadly warnings make it clear that even Ruth is not immune to the encroaching danger....

If great tales are your motive,
make Worldwide Mystery your partner in crime.
Available September 2001 at your favorite retail outlet.

WNMW395